I0602036

OD & ED

A NOVEL

SHANTI LEONARD

FASTENTILT

PRESS

FASTENTILT
PRESS

First hardback edition June 2021
First paperback edition June 2021

Book cover illustration by Xavier Comas
Map by Jennifer Scrobe

www.shantileonard.com

1 3 5 7 9 10 8 6 4 2

ISBN 978-1-7369683-0-7 (hardback)
ISBN 978-1-7369683-1-4 (paperback)
ISBN 978-1-7369683-2-1 (ebook)

To find the truth you must look everywhere...
...even in the dark...where the *things* hide.

This book is for my mom, my dad, my brother, and my sister…for when we used to all be together…and for the house on North Old Stage.

Od and Ed

OCTOBER 1988

PERFECTS

"WE CAN DO WEIRD THINGS," said Odlyn Perfect.

It was daytime, but all the lights were off. Strange things could happen in a house with all the lights off, when long-loved colors were thrown into gray, and stray spears of sunlight stabbed forgotten pieces of molding and carpet. Sound and thought would bend in crooked ways and whatever lingering blitheness you had inside would fold up and stick in your sides. It was a *different* place.

Od chewed the inside of her cheek. "Ed can make things move…" her eyes darted out to meet her brother's and then returned to Bernie, "…with his mind."

They all sat together, tailor-style, on Od's bed. The comforter was thrown loosely over the rumples in a lumpy pink mass, hiding all the pillows, dolls, and plush figures that lived there. Od's floor-clothes and toy debris were crammed against the wall, creating a narrow path of shag carpet that almost made the room appear cleaner than it actually was.

"It's not with my mind really…" Edwyn Perfect was being contrary as he was prone to do. He flicked his head to the side, cracking his neck just like their father. "It's hard to explain."

Ed reached toward Melvin, Od's stuffed white monkey. Ed twitched as if a familiar pain crept into him that he had to constantly shove away. Bernie looked at the Monkey.

Did it move?

Bernie frowned and squinted against the dim of the room, pushing his head out toward the chair to confirm what he had just seen. Ed squinted along with him, head cocked to the side, hand still out, reaching for Melvin's stitched mouth, long arms, and Velcro palms. His nylon fur, once smooth and straight, was matted from a former trip to the dryer.

The monkey raised its arm.

A noise leapt into the room from the back of Bernie's throat, somewhere between a gasp and a squeal. Something inexplicable exploded within him and ran along his limbs. It coursed up his neck, giving him goosebumps, and making him feel light and scared. As the explosion melted away, it left him feeling strong.

"Don't tell," Edwyn commanded and the monkey's arm dropped back down. "We would have never told you except for, well, we think you might be able to do stuff like this. Move things. Tether things. More, maybe. I'm not sure how it works. It's as if our imagination is bleeding into reality."

"Stop trying to figure it out," said Od. "It isn't going to work anymore if you do that."

Ed frowned at his sister. "That doesn't make any sense," he said. "Why wouldn't it work if I figured it out?"

"I think the power is connected to the mystery of it," she said.

"Kind of like how the Roadrunner doesn't fall because he doesn't look down?" Ed made a half smile that only he could make, and winked at Bernie.

"The Roadrunner's a *girl*," said Od and Ed rolled his eyes.

Bernie thought of his cat, Bigfoot. He was forced to give her to his brother after what had happened. *Maybe I could give Bigfoot back her eye with this magic.* Maybe Hell didn't await him for what he had done.

"It's not *magic*," Od said. "It's just learning how to make things happen."

Did she hear *him think the word "magic" in his head or was that a coincidence?* He sure hoped it was a coincidence. Sometimes he had thoughts about her in there. And she was his own *cousin.* He felt his face go hot. "I want to do it," Bernie said. "The uh, not-magic."

Edwyn looked at Bernie. "Open the drawer."

Bernie started to get up.

"No, *open* it."

Bernie looked from one pair of Perfect eyes to the other.

He reached out like Edwyn did and shook in a forced twitch. Ed had done that. *"It's not with my mind really..."* Bernie imagined a ghost-arm sliding out of his own pudgy hand and across the gray room, grabbing the knob, *it was shiny and cool,* pulling at it...it moved...cracked...opened... *Oh shit! Odlyn's underwear drawer!* He lost his concentration. None of them were falling out or anything, but he knew they were in there. He knew that there was one less pair too. Pink, green, and white, striped ones. *Did I open the drawer because of that?* No, Ed had meant that one, he had *pointed* to that drawer. The drawer stopped moving.

"Wow," Edwyn said. "Od didn't even do it that quick."

Bernie did it. He did the not-magic. The heat from the realization of what drawer he was opening was still in his face, but the rest of the world changed. It had expanded, and at the same time it narrowed down to a pinprick. Things were going to be different now. He was somebody.

Something snapped in the room.

It was a deep snap that sucked part of the air out and replaced it with something else. It snapped again. In the closet. The ceiling. Below. Above. A snap that enveloped everything; that came from behind everywhere. A sickening snap that ran through his guts and into his bones.

Odlyn stood up. "You have to go."

"What?" Bernie said.

Odlyn looked into his eyes. Edwyn was holding his head. "You need to leave. Don't tell anyone about this. Not your brother, not Carrie, not our parents, or yours, or *anyone's* parents. Nobody. Got it?" There was a soft rumble and Od's eyes went to the closet. "It's mad."

Bernie ran.

2

OD

OD STOPPED HERSELF from tugging at the waist of her jeans. She wasn't a Perfect—not by blood, at least. Her hair was pale, her eyes dirt gray, so un-Perfect. "What's it so mad at?"

"I don't know," Ed said as he climbed into the closet, sat down, and closed his eyes.

Od picked up a ukulele. Dust motes danced around the strings as she picked through them with her fingers. The sound was boxy and bright—not a song though, mostly just notes scraping against each other along a minor scale.

Od's ears popped and she could hear better. The immediacy in the air evaporated and some normalcy dripped in. The uncertainty that hung when the house *thinned* or *thickened* made it feel like everything could cave-in on itself, like the fabric of everything could rip and things could tumble through and get you. But for now, the house calmed.

Ed was the one who did it. He had a way with it. He could click himself off, plug in, and calm it. The ukulele sometimes helped Ed click off and plug in. It was something to *drift* to, he said. Od thought that it might not help him at all, that maybe it was just something Ed told her so that she felt like she was helping.

Ed came back on. His eyes opened and stared at nothing. He twitched again, this movement more natural than the one earlier. Od quickly plugged her ears, pinning the bits of cartilage against her earholes with her fingers, and Ed screamed until he ran out of breath. She had to cover his face with a pillow once when their parents were home and they had to calm the house. She felt weird doing it, especially since Ed never remembered the scream, but she didn't know what else to do.

They weren't sure exactly why the house would get mad. They had guesses for specific times when it occurred. Too many lights on. People it didn't like were visiting. Too many fires or candles going. But this time, Od couldn't guess why.

"Ughhhh." Ed rubbed his eyes with his knuckles as he climbed out of the closet. "You wanna get some pizza?"

"Uh, doi."

Od always wanted to get some pizza.

SEEING as though neither of them was even near old enough to drive legally, nor have a car at their disposal, they biked into town. The ride was about forty minutes; down the long twisted road they lived on, left on Crest, past the gray houses, past the church and the cemetery, across the bridge over the freeway, past the hospital and Timber Hills Elementary, then right, then left, and finally into the main shopping center where The Pizza Parlor was.

They leaned their bikes against the wall just outside. "Was that mean?" Od said.

"Huh?"

"What we did to Bernie?"

"Nah, just bad timing," Ed said. "I mean, wouldn't you think it was cool if we did it to you?" It was a great idea, rigging the room with fishing line. While it was Ed's idea, he had wanted to tell Bernie it was a ghost. It was Od's idea to convince him that the Perfects had magical powers.

"Yeah, but we didn't tell him that it was fake," Od said.

"That's because the house got mad," Ed said. "We'll tell him later. He'll get pissed for a couple seconds and then think it was awesome and say we should do it to his brother." It was kind of weird, pretending to do magic in a house that was *wrong*. There was something *funny* about it, although that wasn't quite the right word. Nobody knew that there were… things that infested the house except for Od and Ed, and that those things could potentially fall out.

THE SOUNDS OF THE ARCADE melted into a cold pixelated soup, which Od drank in and separated in her mind. There were the electric chimes and coin splashes from *Dragon's Lair*; a steady voice permeating throughout, a high-pitched metamorphosis scream from *Altered Beast*, gravelly punches and kicks from *Double Dragon*, and somebody was hitting the brakes way too much on *OutRun*. Synthesized and lo-bit themes battled each other. The deep clacks and robotic scales from the pinballs bouncing around the innards, of both *PIN·BOT* and *High Speed*, kept a chaotic beat. And "Every Little Counts" by New Order was playing on the jukebox.

The Pizza Parlor had the biggest arcade in town. Which wasn't saying much, since the town of Timber Hills only had a fall-total of 3,212 people. But it also had the best pizza in the county, which was saying a bit more. The competition was a bit fierce pizza-wise in Chinook County. However, there were only two other true contenders for the crown as far as Od and most playground epicures were concerned. One was Stanley's Pizza Factory in Strawberry Valley, about thirty miles away. The other was Good Knight Pizza in Dunsmore, the next town over. Neither held a crumb to The Pizza Parlor.

"What if we could rig the whole house up with fishing line

and stuff and have somebody come in and go through it? Make like a story or something they had to figure out," said Ed.

Od didn't look up from the cabinet, but she smiled. "Would we tell them it was fake?" She had gone for two levels now without losing a life.

"I think we would have to," Ed admitted.

She could see Ed peripherally, but focused on the screen. Maybe he was teasing her, or even testing her video-gaming skills with the distraction. Od let her mind fill with puzzles and stories that could be seeded into the house. She wondered if the house would bend the game they made inside it somehow, twist it in some way to fit its desires. Or would the game just make it mad? The only way to find out though would be to create it.

It would start with the front door. There would be a note tucked into the worn brass handle-set hinting on how you were supposed to knock to unlock the door. So Ed would have to be on one side of the door and Od the other when somebody came to experience the House Game. She should be the one inside, behind the scenes, and working behind the puzzles. When they figured out that first puzzle with the door knock she would unlock the door and move, unnoticed, to the--

--GOBLIN!

--She tapped the jump button, but may have done it a little too lightly, because her avatar did not jump. The low computerized *drip-drop* sounded and her avatar fell off the screen. One life down. She definitely didn't hit the button late. "I pressed the button! Come on!" She shook her head and tucked her hair behind her ears. "This game cheats." She had totally pressed the button.

"Take two," said Ed.

The game restarted her in a section where she had almost no choice but to die immediately. So she died and then laughed.

"OK, *that* time it cheated," Ed said.

"Edwyn. Pizza for Edwyn." Their compromise-pizza was ready and Ed left without saying anything to go get it. If he had his druthers he would have had one of the nastiest pizzas known to the world: shrimp and onion. If Od had it her way, she would get extra cheese and pineapple. As always, mushroom and olive was the middle ground. Ed said that they could do half shrimp and onion and half cheese and pineapple, but when those grody little shrimps were baked into the cheese it ruined the whole pizza.

Od started again and hopped the goblin with a forceful slap of the jump button. She paused. Jumped and threw some axes. She was on the last bridge of the level when spikes rained down upon her. The castle stones melted into spectres and engulfed her. *Drip-drop*. Game over. She pulled the queued quarter off the glass and put it back in her pocket. That game cheated. She just knew it.

ED HAD FOUND A SPOT IN THE BACK next to the dragon mural where he was already inhaling a slice. Od sat down, filled a plastic tumbler with Coke, took a swig, and scraped a sheet of cheese and toppings off a slice. She tossed the rest of it back onto the metal pan it had been served on.

Ed picked up Od's discarded triangle of crust and fit it neatly under a fresh slice, creating a sort of double-crust pizza. That move had saved Od from getting in trouble more than a few times. "Got any good what-ifs?" Ed smiled.

"Hmmm…" she said and bit the inside of her cheek. She and Ed had a tradition of coming up with elaborate what-if scenarios for the other to answer. It was one of her favorite things to do with Ed, but it took some work to do it right. She had a few half-formed what-ifs floating in her head, but nothing complete. She sighed. "I can't think of one right now. Maybe on our ride back." She crunched on mouthful of Coke-flavored ice pellets. Why any restaurant chose ice cubes over ice pellets was one of life's great mysteries.

"Alright, better be a good one."

Od grabbed another slice.

"OK, if you could have one wish, what would it be?" Ed asked.

"Infinity wishes."

Ed looked at his sister as he chewed a big mouthful of cheese, sauce, and mushrooms. "Ass," he said.

Od smiled. "What? Tell me a wish that's better." She knew he couldn't, but she wasn't really playing fair.

"Fine," he said and took another bite. "If you could have any *power*, like magic power, what would it be?"

"The power to generate an infinite number of wishes." Od held a laugh in and picked at some cheese.

Ed shook his head. "Ass."

Od scraped the rest of the cheese and toppings from her second slice and abandoned another "crust plate" to the tray. "One power... to be able to fly, I guess."

"Fine," Ed said. "But you have to run really fast and flap your arms really hard to do it. And you can normally only get a few feet off the ground. Sometimes you can get higher, but not consistently. Would you *still* pick flying?"

Od laughed. "No."

"So, what then?" Now Ed wasn't playing fair.

"What would *you* pick, then?" Od said.

"There was this supervillain named The Creeper." Ed wiped his mouth with the back of his hand and then, when he saw the back of his hand, he wiped it with a napkin. "He could strike fear into his foes or make them go crazy or go into a coma." He took a big bite and with his mouth full added, "With his laugh."

Od rolled her eyes. "That's so stupid."

"If you can control fear, you can make people do *anything*."

"But what if you go see a stand-up comedian and start laughing? He'd get all scared and not be able to finish his jokes. Or if you were at school and somebody did something you thought was funny, everybody would be dropping into comas and going crazy."

Ed started laughing and Od spasmed on cue. She crossed her eyes and let her head fall with a *thunk* to the table. She closed her eyes and lay still for a couple seconds. Then she opened one eye to see Ed's reaction. He didn't even acknowledge it. "I think I'd have control over the laugh. Like it would be a special laugh. Not my regular, haha-that's-funny laugh," he said.

"It would be a much cooler power if your laugh just made you float to the ceiling."

"Very funny." That meant he didn't think it was funny.

Od started picking off another slice of pizza. "If you could have the power of being invisible..." She looked up at him. "Good power, right?"

He reluctantly agreed. "Yeah."

"If you could be invisible whenever you wanted, but all of the food you ever ate would taste like broccoli to you... Would you do it?"

"All the time, or just when I was invisible?" Ed was thorough.

"All the time." Of course. Ed frowned and started to think.

"Oh... drinks too?" he asked.

"You can choose two drinks that can taste normal. Everything else tastes like broccoli water. Would you do it?" Od said.

"No way," Ed said. Then he thought for a moment. "Well..."

"I would," Od said.

"How 'bout this," Ed said. "You can have the ability to tell when anyone is lying. By the smell. When they lie, it's the worst smell ever. Like the Bog of Eternal Stench caliber stink. You smell that any time someone lies."

Od thought a second. "I couldn't go anywhere," she said. "Everywhere would smell horrible." She eyed the dragon mural behind Ed. "What about movies?"

"What do you mean?"

"Like if people in movies were lying, could I smell it? Or does it have to be in person?"

Ed considered the question and then said, "I don't think it makes sense to smell it through a screen. They have to be there, in person. Maybe there's a gas or something that comes out of their pores when they lie."

"Movies would be my solace. A big room of quiet people." Od snagged another slice. "If you can't talk, you can't lie."

"Dude, you'd kill people that talk during movies."

"Without remorse."

"You know what would happen? You would be in a movie and somebody would fart and you would think that you could smell the lies in the movie." They both laughed.

"Only if it was an SBDF," Od said as she flayed a final slice of pizza. "Would the smells be different?"

"You mean depending on how bad the lie was?"

"No. I'd assume that however big the lie was the worse the smell would be, but I mean would different people have different-smelling lies?"

"Hey it's your power, Smell-Ra." Ed turned one side of his lips up in a smile, the way he did when he was making a reference to something, or a joke he didn't think somebody would get. She got it. Smell-Ra was supposed to be like She-Ra, but the joke sucked so she ignored both the reference and the look.

"Otherwise, I could be in a room with a bunch of people lying and not know who it was."

"The smell would be coming off them, remember. You could tell that way."

"I still think that everyone's lies would smell a bit different from each other."

"Like B.O.," Ed said.

"What?"

"Like how everyone's B.O. smells different."

"It does?" Od squinted.

"Yeah... doesn't it?"

"I don't think so."

"L.O."

"'Ello to you too, gub'ner."

"Haha, no. L period. O period. Lie odor."

Od laughed.

ED

ED SLAMMED THE PEDALS BACKWARD to brake his Mongoose and carved up the gravel driveway, leaving a line of dark dirt in the bike's wake. It was a good one too, long and deep. He swung his leg off the bike and turned to cover the dirt back up with rocks but stopped—he had plenty of time to fix it by tomorrow morning and he might want to make a couple more skid marks before then.

He turned back toward the steepled house—and for some reason, today, in that moment, it struck him as it never had. Ed had always thought of it as a Gothic gingerbread house of sorts, but just then, the way it stabbed into the cinereal sky, enclosed in the porous pickets of a beaten gray fence, it seemed a new edifice: a church of some obscure religion. It inspired awe and a feeling not too different from fright in his chest. He noticed Od surveying him and looked back at her. The amoeba-shaped pool, which hadn't been cleaned since his ninth birthday, reflected in her eyes. It threw beryl shines dancing across those silver discs. Sometimes they were hard not to look at. And sometimes he thought that having a twin would not be too different from how he felt about Od.

Thick emotions splayed across the space between him and the house, climbing up his body and seeping into him. Moments passed in skips, like a needle bouncing between grooves on a record. He hadn't realized he was running until he was halfway there. He could hear his heart thumping somewhere between his ears and throat. The front door was flying open.

Inside it was like those fight-dreams where Loony Scrobe was right in front of him and Ed was swinging as hard as he could, but his arms would barely move. Like in a video game, when there was too much to process on-screen, and the engine couldn't keep up.

He tripped down the entryway and slid across the kitchen floor, down the hall, and into his room. Ed pulled open his closet door and sat in amongst the toys. He turned himself off and clicked into the house.

It grabbed his heart and curled up inside of him. His arms went behind his torso and he leaned back on his wrists, hands palm up on the floor. His back was opening up in the way it usually did, countless knives cutting up his spine. It was more aggressive than before though, and it was making him cold…a feeling he hadn't felt since forever.

Ed was aware of music… then it all went blank.

HE OPENED HIS EYES TO FIND OD. The uke was hanging out of her left hand. He didn't know how long he had been in the closet, and he could hear…*himself?*…saying something, but Od couldn't understand him. Maybe he was just mouthing the words. Yes, that was it. But he couldn't remember how to make sounds. He couldn't remember what he was trying to say. He fell backwards from trying to speak, back into the house, and his body suddenly remembered how to talk. It had something to say.

"Scarebox!"

SCAREBOX

THE HOLE FELT DEEPER SOMEHOW and Od was almost up to her shoulder. She had never had to reach so far before, *had* she? But then her fingers found it.

The scarebox.

For a second, just a second, she thought that she shouldn't use it, but the doubt was overridden by desperation and panic, and she was pulling it out into the light. It was about the size of a shoebox, and roughly a square, but too heavy for its apparent size.

They had found the box three summers ago, hidden under a trick in the floor. There had been instructions in a black envelope fastened to the lid.

In case of emergency:
When the House cannot be quieted,
open the scarebox.

To open: Press Brass Button

CAUTION:
There may be
deathly
side effects.

Od sat tailor-fashion in front of Ed with the box in her lap. She could feel the raised grain of the ruddy-black box and the worn brass button set in the dark wood. Ed sat on a mound of his jeans and t-shirts in the closet, nestled amongst piles of action figures and playsets. Two halves of Castle Grayskull lay on either side of him, almost as if he had been inside the castle and eaten the wrong side of the mushroom, growing, and splitting the castle in twain.

He had been trying to calm the house for too long. His eyes were shut and flicking back and forth under their lids. The house's air was mixed, thick and thin, making possibility seem upside down, and the world itself shimmery and unstable.

Od's neck went cold, and goosebumps covered her arms. Ed's eyes stopped moving and the lids darkened, as if his eyes had fallen back into his head and the space between was being filled with blood. She would regret the decision many times after this, but at the moment there didn't seem to be another. So she pressed the button.

OUT

ED WASN'T COLD, LIKE ALWAYS. He had a disorder that kept him from experiencing the feeling, or that is what they told him. It was also the reason he had to have blood taken out of his body on a regular basis. Not for blood tests, but because iron would build up in his body and the only way to get it out was to remove some of his blood. Ed once asked what they did with that blood after they took it out, since he believed that *he* owned it, but nobody could ever give him a straight answer. The not-feeling-cold thing was not a common side effect; in fact, from what he heard it was an anomaly, and sometimes it made him feel like he had a superpower. *This* not-feeling-cold though was different. It wasn't just an absence of cold—it was loss of all sensation. He could feel himself losing…*everything*, falling…*out* of himself…backward. His hands slipped off like gloves, and his feet like shoes that you were supposed to eventually grow into. His chest fell out, and his head came undone. He slid away, back and away…away from life… from himself, from thought and light, and dark, and all. His consciousness faded, thin as the first freeze on their pool.

He felt a dull *plunk* as he separated from his body, and saturation drained from everything. He could see Od with the scarebox still open on her lap, darkness storming from it, scaring all away. The storm whipped against his body. A body that wasn't part of him anymore, a body that sat still in the closet before him.

He moved forward…or thought to…but he could only drift. He drifted backward, limbs sprawling in slow motion, almost like those fight-dreams. His body's head moved. *So strange to think of my body as a separate thing.* Then Od and his body faded away. He reached for them, but again, it was only a thought. *Was it a thought if it wasn't in my head?* His actual self, his *ghost*—or whatever he was now—wouldn't respond. Or maybe it was responding, but it was too slow to have any effect. The room faded too, all passing away into a shining gray of *nothing*.

GRAVE CIRCUMSTANCES

OD SHUT THE SCAREBOX. It didn't seem to have done anything. Although now there was a faint smell of dirt and something else too faint to put a word to. Ed's eyes were open now, though. Od shoved her fingers into her ears, waiting for him to scream.

Ed was getting up. He didn't scream—he just glanced at Od with her fingers in her ears, frowned, and walked out the door. Od followed him down the hall, through the kitchen, through the entryway and out the front door. "Ed!" He kept going, leaving the door wide open. She grabbed him. "Dude, what's up?" He stared at her with vague disinterest.

"What?" he asked.

"What are you doing? What happened?"

He looked at her with nothing behind his eyes and walked off toward the street. She grabbed his hand and he turned toward her, but then he noticed the Mongoose and shook her off. He picked up his bike, got on, and pedaled away.

"ED!"

Od grabbed her bike and followed him. He rode in the car lane, instead of off to the side, no matter what Od yelled at him. Cars passed, two of which honked, one of which had somebody inside that yelled. Od saw Sarah Snow in the back of the last one, rolling her eyes at thirty-five miles an hour.

Od followed him down the twisted road they lived on, left on

Crest, past the gray houses, and then Ed turned into the graveyard.

The grass was longer and sparser in the front, with dirt patches and giant pines. The gravestones were weathered, some un-readable, cracked, or crumbling. Ed ignored this part and rode to the back. The trees thinned the farther back they went, eventually giving way to a field of gravestones stippled with younger trees, then to a manicured lawn with a grid of rectangle grave-plates. There he jumped off his bike, letting it ghost ride until it crashed between a couple of those death plaques, and then he sat in the grass.

Od got off her bike and laid it in on the grass next to a grave marker that read,

Jerome Jennings
Beloved Husband
"Child of Destiny"

"What are you doing?" Od asked.

"Sitting."

She chewed the inside of her cheek. "Sitting?"

And that was what he did. He just sat there until it started to get dark, no matter what Od said or did. She thought of calling their parents, but that wouldn't do any good. They were too far away to do anything, and if she did call them they might just call Carrie, Od and Ed's aunt, who they were supposed to contact if something bad happened while their parents were away. Od would rather sleep in the graveyard with Ed than have to deal with that woman. Even if they did come home from the city, she'd have to try to explain about the box again, a tale that they did not believe. She had tried to tell them about it before, against Ed's advice, and they thought she was just "making up a story." That's what her mother called lies. The woman seemed to think that even the word "lies" was an obscenity. She had heard her mother call someone a liar once before and it was the most venomous thing Od had ever heard from her mouth. Plus, if they came home now, her mom would see that her room was still a mess.

She tried to talk to Ed a dozen different ways, gave him a couple decent what-ifs she thought up on the spot, asked him questions, tried to be mean or sad or whatever she could think up, but it didn't work. She was thinking she might actually have to sleep out there with Ed when she saw a gravestone that made her think of Loney Scrobe.

The gravestone had a poem on it that reminded her of the one Emily Chetel used to say about Loney.

Lovely Laura "Luna" Lemon
As Tall as a Tree
Surely in Heaven

Loney, who Emily called "Loony", lived on a street a short bike ride from Od's house in the opposite direction of the graveyard. It was an eerie crooked street that Od always ended up riding down, since it was less than a block away, had almost no traffic, and was certified safe by her parents. It didn't feel safe though, and when riding certain parts of it she would always be compelled to go faster to get away from something she could not quite describe.

All of the houses on Wisner Road were disturbed. There was no rhyme or reason to how they were positioned, which way they faced, or how far they were from the street. And each was their own special version of wrong. Loney's house was no different, and Od didn't want to go there, but she knew *somehow* that Loney could get Ed out of the graveyard, so she went. She pedaled past her own house and turned right onto Wisner, the poem about

Loony running in her head as she went.

> *Lonely Loony Loney Scrobe*
> *Comes to school in his bathrobe*
> *Smells like cheese*
> *And pee*
> *And mold*
> *Lonely Loony Loney Scrobe.*

The bit about the pee and mold was nonsense, although there was a distinct smell to "Loony" that she couldn't quite place. It wasn't necessarily unpleasant, but she would hardly call it endearing. The bathrobe thing happened twice, which Od didn't understand at all, and Loney did always have a rather large hunk of cheese in his lunch each day.

THE SCROBE LAND was a broad flat stretch with two large, empty fields out front sloping up to the street. A dirt drive ran between the fields, peeling off the back hill of Wisner at a right angle. Od pedaled down it on Ed's Mongoose. He wasn't going to use it right now anyway, and if he did finally decide to go home he could ride hers—it'd serve him right. She passed by several holes in the back of the right field, the dirt around them sprayed with sudden brownish flecks. She looked away. There was a rumor about cats involving "Loony" that matched that sight. She made herself not believe it for the time being and pedaled harder towards the house. The holes could have spawned the stories just as easily as they could have proven rumors.

There were two buildings of some sort behind the fields, wrapped in aluminum siding, that Od was forced to ride between to get to the house. She could feel the heat that had been stored from the day pouring off the metal on each side as she passed and she made sure to ride dead center until she came out the other side into an empty space. Behind that space was a short bluish house with a single step leading to its front door.

Od swung her leg off the Mongoose and dropped the bike next to something black that might have been a tree once. She walked up to the door, wanting to run the other way, but she was pinned to it by obligation. *Don't go on! This is not the way! Take heed and go no further. Beware! Beware! Soon it will be too late.* The false alarms echoed in her head like words in a hidden passage behind a darkened oubliette. She knocked. *Doesn't want his ring back in his mouth, huh? Can't say I blame 'im.* Some movies were just burned into her mind, spitting up random bits of lines or music whenever her unconscious tied a connection to the moment.

Od knew that Loony—*no, not Loony, it's Loney, I can't call him that*—she knew that *Loney* liked her. Everyone at school knew. How could they not, when he went to school with that shirt on? That *shirt*! Did he really think that wearing it would have any kind of desirable outcome? And how did he think it was going to make all the other kids act towards *her*? At least her anger drowned out her fear for a second. She knocked harder, which admittedly wasn't very hard at all.

Corlan opened the door, gray hair sticking out of his beanie in stiff straw-like strands. He was the oldest Scrobe kid, and as tall as Od's dad, even though he was only in ninth grade. When he saw Od he didn't say anything, he just laughed down at her and walked off, leaving the door open to the dark of the Scrobe living room. An old wooden television set, probably near three hundred pounds, was on, playing a court show of some type for absolutely no one, and at the far end of the room was a fluorescent pale hallway that hooked away out of sight. The only other obvious exit was the walkway to the right that Corlan had disappeared through.

She thought about knocking again on the open door, but was

afraid of making too much noise and attracting Loney's younger brother, Gatch. It might also alert whatever had spawned the Scrobe kids to her presence and Od realized very suddenly that she did not want to do that. *Who would ever name their kid Gatch?*

So Od stepped in, a slight draft pushing at her back as she took that first step onto the thin, cheap carpet. The colorless hallway across the room from her was bathed in a gross artificial light that left harsh shadows. She started for it, but after a couple steps got the feeling that she was a bug flying toward a zapper, so she followed Corlan.

The walkway to the right held some cupboards, a shelf, and a side doorway that led to more darkness, but soon it opened into the kitchen, which was, of course, the scariest room of the house.

The kitchen was a dull arylide yellow. Maybe it had been bright once, but now it looked sick. Gray stuck to the cabinets, over the intended yellow, to the fridge, the ceiling, and the swirly brown and white linoleum. It stuck to the wooden table that dominated the room, and it even seemed to stick to the boys sitting around it in mismatched chairs. Unfortunately they were all there: Corlan, Gatch, Thad, Bray, and Loney.

In the center of the table was a board game. It looked legitimate enough, with a semi-gloss shine and a crease in the board itself from being folded and stored, but Od had never seen it before, which was weird since Od secretly thought of herself as a board game connoisseur.

Big illustrations bedecked the board in a broad Saturday-morning cartoon style. Monsters crawled forth from a coiled smoke border that melted into dripping colors at the bottom. A parchment colored path wound back and forth until reaching what appeared to be the goal: an actual plastic house perched atop a plastic hill. At the top of the house was a clichéd Dracula-esque vampire head with slicked hair, a gaping mouth, and pointy eyebrows. The game pieces were ghosts and skeletons, differentiated only by their colors. After counting Od assumed that they must all be playing two pieces; one skeleton and one ghost each.

The boys were all staring at her. Thad, the least strange of them, spoke first. He was a grade ahead of her and *almost* fit in at school. "Hi, Odlyn. Play." He fished out a yellow skeleton from a tapered hexagonal box and held it out. Strange…she *did* want to play. She loved board games, but rarely got a chance to play with a bunch of kids, and the last time Od had played one she'd never seen before was at Sarah Snow's house. It was called Stop Thief! and it had a handheld electronic device that gave you hints as to where the thief was sneaking about. That game was good for the novelty. *This* game looked like it might be as good as Crossbows and Catapults. Which was saying a lot.

"Uh, I need to talk to Loney," she said.

Loney, who had been trying to look anywhere but at Od, finally looked at her.

A couple of the Scrobes laughed. Thad and Bray made that TV "woooo" sound a studio audience made when people started kissing.

"OK," said Thad, "but first you have to play the *Vampire Game*." When he said, "Vampire Game" he made a dumb spooky voice and arched his eyebrows.

"It's kinda important that I talk to him," she said.

"So is the Vampire Game," said one of the boys.

"Come on." She definitely didn't want to go into it with the other Scrobe boys. For sure Loney was weird and awkward, but he lacked the recklessness his brothers had the true I-don't-give-a-fuck attitude that so many kids played at. If she told them all what was going on they'd all go running over to her house and then to the graveyard. They'd make things worse even if she stressed the importance of it, probably more so because of the importance to her. Od thought of Katie Cooper. When Od did something that Katie thought was making something worse she sometimes said, rather snarkily, "Why don't you just invite a Scrobe over?" Od thought that the phrase was mean for no real good reason, but Katie had a point.

"What's so important?" asked Thad.

She did her best to look like she was hiding a blush, like maybe she came over to ask Loney to go out with her, but she didn't think she was doing it very well. Od had a rule for herself to never lie. She could imply something, or twist meanings slightly, just as long as she never said something that was untrue. It was best not to tell anyone about that rule, she learned, but it did guide her. "It's private."

"Just play the game," said Thad.

She sighed. "How long does it take?"

"Fifteen minutes."

She sighed. "Fine."

The game was weird. There were dice shaped like bones and others shaped like pyramids with only four sides. Sometimes when you rolled the bone dice you moved the other player's skeletons instead of your own and sometimes you drew cards from a tray called the Grave Pit. Part of the goal was to stay away from the house and part of it was completely unclear to Od. There were traps and Fate cards and a graveyard that acted as a type of jail. She was right about everyone having two game pieces, but for some reason she only got one. When she asked about it, they just said that it would take longer if she played "with a soul." She found that hard to believe, since they had already been playing for what seemed like an hour. Maybe they were just playing Calvinball.

"This is taking forever," she said.

Gatch rolled the dice and smiled. "Fine," he said and moved her piece to the front of the little house. His smile looked like a disease spreading across his face.

"So, what now? I lost?"

"Now you have to stick your finger in the vampire's mouth."

They all stared.

"And then it's game over for you."

The Dracula-like head stared at her with its blank red orbs, plastic hair reflecting the overhead light. Behind its tiny teeth the light fell away and was replaced with a sudden and muddy darkness. The boys looked on, all their faces like plastic reflections mirroring the immortal head perched on the little game house. She put her finger in its mouth. They all leaned forward. Gatch was smiling. Was Loney nervous? Thad got up. "You need to put it in all the way. Until you can feel the back…" Od shook her head, but still pushed her finger further into the head, past the teeth and into the darkness. She thought she felt the back with her fingernail, pushed a little further. Something clicked and the jaws snapped shut on her finger. She jumped.

The boys laughed. It didn't really hurt, and the head opened immediately to release her finger, but she did jump, big time. Hopefully she didn't scream too. Od looked at her finger as it began to itch…and two tiny marks appeared on her finger, then they blossomed into dots of actual blood.

"What the fuck!" Od said and sucked her finger. The Scrobes all laughed.

7

THE PALE

HE WAS STILL IN THE SHINING GRAY. His sister and his body were gone, but gray ghosts of furniture and the long pale curtains of walls remained. The off-white shadows of his toys still lay as he had left them, carpeting the floor of his tiny closet. It seemed bigger now, maybe because Ed was at the back of the closet, stuck halfway in and out of the wall. There was a word stuck in his head, like a song he hadn't heard the ending to. *Focus.* The word seemed to battle his natural state in this place. He felt distance and a new crooked apathy. Everything was unsaturated, even his thoughts. There was another thing stuck in his head, a knowledge that he should not go into *the doors*, and a half-thought that he should use the *tunnels*. Neither knowledge made much sense to him.

Things floated in the air, covered in gray-ish clumps that made them unrecognizable. Some of these things drifted and disappeared as they got too far away. Some just hung there, spinning slightly or simply fading away. A pale clung to it all. A paleness that was not unlike clouds. And not unlike mucus.

Walking was difficult. His limbs were heavy, but floating, and some of those pale *things* that stuck to him slowed him down. Bits of that cloud-mucus swam through the air in random lines and attached themselves to his shirt. *Hmm... I'm still wearing a shirt,* Ed thought. *Guess my soul had a shirt.* Without thinking, he brushed some of the cloud-mucus off of himself with clumsy ghost arms. Some of it came off in wisps, some of it dripped away, and some rolled up into tiny snail-like spirals and dropped to the pale beneath him. The *pale* was getting thicker, making it difficult to tell where he was. He forced himself to move, partly stomping, partly floating, toward the hall. It was similar to floating in a lake and trying to walk at the same time, with the lake floor too far beneath to make much contact with.

A dog walked down the hall toward him, having no trouble with the pale world at all. In his disorientation and apathy Ed almost forgot that this particular dog, Steven Spielberg, had been dead for a year.

Focus. The word was still there, playing over again in his head. Not a word—a feeling.

Ed tried to say something to the dog, but only a dry gasp came out. He knelt down to ruffle the fur behind Steven Spielberg's big shaggy ears and accidentally sunk his hands into the ghost dog's head. It was dense and soft. He pulled his fingers out once he noticed what had happened and the dog let out a gurgling type of yelp. Mucus dripped and wisped from Ed's hands as they came loose. His dog's head was malformed now, lopsided, with a jaw that had now come undone. Ed felt his apathy twisting into some type of incomprehensible emotion and then Steven Spielberg lost more of his shape and melted into the gray.

Ed stumbled further into the hallway. Just as in the living world, tall mirrors lined either side from end to end. But here, instead of reflections, light and shadows moved behind their glass. Each seemed to be alive. Each a door to where something else dwelled. At the far end and to the right, where a closet should have been, was instead a dark void. Ed had once taken a trip to the lava tubes with his scout troop. When they had climbed a quarter mile inside, they all turned their flashlights off. It was a darkness that he never experienced before or after: the complete absence of light. This void made that darkness look like a color of the rainbow. Ed backed away as quickly as he could, continuing back down the hallway, past the kitchen, and into the house's entryway. The front door of the house was bright, glowing whiter than white. No…not white…*light,* a hypnotic visceral light that Ed could not fit any words around. Not blinding to look at, but dynamic. To his left was the living room, sunken and alive. Bits of pale were floating everywhere. The furniture was so covered with the stuff that they just looked like mounds of ill snow. The corner where his mom kept her dolls was a pile of writhing, humanoid shapes, all crawling and climbing around each other, shifting from side to side and top to bottom. *I knew those things were alive.*

Ed backed away, stomping and floating into the kitchen, and that's when he saw *her*. She was sitting on the stove and both her and the stove were glowing red. She was glowing too brightly to be sure, but he could have sworn she wasn't wearing anything. As she got up, the wood-burning stove dimmed and her own redness cracked and fell away. Now she wore a white dress. Her skin was thin and he could see what looked like fire moving underneath it. She walked easily toward Ed. Then through him. And she was gone.

In the den, roosting from pale, lumpy dunes and watching him with ashen-black eyes, was every cat they had ever owned. Even the little one Od got when she first came to the house was there. Ed was glad to see him again. It was strange to see something from back when he found Od alone in that house of other kids. His parents took him there because they wanted him to have a brother, but he chose *her*, a sister. She had been sitting in the back of that room, her bright blonde hair cut above the shoulders. She was kind of like his negative copy. He couldn't tell if she was older than him, or younger, but he knew right away that she was stronger. When they started talking, they found that they both had the same weird quirks. Similar names. Tastes. Later they found out that they had the same birthday, same day, same month, same time, just a different year. They were meant for each other. He knew it right away. Ed slipped out of the memory, happy that Od's little cat was well after what had happened to him in the living world.

After the den Ed looked in each room. Some quiet. Some moving, like the sunken living room. When Ed saw the glowing girl again, she was in her little white dress and he couldn't stop looking at her legs. The dress was short and moving. She wasn't glowing, but something about her made him still think of fire. Then she said—well, nothing out loud—but she pushed emotions at him, almost like the pure meaning behind a word. A loose blend of emotions unrolled upon him, part joy, part respect, part strength. He thought it meant, "hi."

Ed tried to say hi back, but it came out as a dry rasp closer to "grrah." She laughed at his attempt, but it was less an audible laugh and more a visual one, containing light and feeling. Another cluster of emotions hit him. Curiosity-sadness-reverence-joy? She was asking him something, but he couldn't understand. Ed tried to talk again. And again it didn't work. The emotions she pushed at him were sweet. They felt new, young. It made him less apathetic and more content. An understated nervous-contentedness hit him. *What was that feeling?* Then a pride with joy and praise, mixed with something heavier, fell against his chest. It felt meaningful, but casual. He almost understood it that time.

Ed tried to go towards her, but when he tried to go into the hallway from the kitchen, for some reason, he ended up back in the sunken living room.

8

ODD KNOWLEDGE

LONEY'S ROOM HAD THREE BEDS. The walls were covered with magazine clippings of pretty girls, movie advertisements from the Sunday paper, and pages from *Nintendo Power*. Loney was moving from foot to foot, leaning against the wall for a couple seconds, then not. He didn't seem to know where to look or how to stand. *How do you communicate with someone who was acting like this?*

"Hey, I think you can help me," said Od.

"OK." He was starting to sit, then decided not to. Maybe this whole thing was a mistake.

"You don't have to feel weird."

Loney finally looked up into her eyes and said, "My brothers made me wear that shirt."

"What?" And then, it kind of made sense.

"They were talking about girls from school and they were all saying who they thought the prettiest was. They held me down and made me say who I thought it was." Loney was looking at his feet and pushing something under one of the beds. She couldn't help but feel…flattered. Even though it was Loney. Even though he wore that shirt to *school*. "They teased me for a long time and then made that shirt and said if I didn't wear it they would cut off my pinky-toes when I was sleeping." Loney dared to look at her again. "Even if they didn't do that, they would have done something… maybe something worse."

She was less flattered for some reason she didn't understand. "Well, I don't care about that. The shirt, I mean." *Anymore. Not really, anyway.* "I think there may be something you can help me with. I don't know why. Maybe because of those drawings you do in class or something you said before—I don't know. I just try to follow my instincts. So..." Od was gearing up to spill it. At least Loney looked a bit more comfortable now. She was just going to say it, matter-of-factly, like she was talking about anything other than this. She took a deep breath.

"So..." Loney found a spot against the wall and leaned against it with his hands in his pockets.

"Something is wrong with Ed."

"What?" It was more of a 'what did you say' than a 'what's wrong with him'. Loney and Ed didn't get along.

"He's not really talking, and he won't leave the graveyard."

"Did someone just die?"

"No, no. He—" *Just say it. Just say it.* "Well, there was this box. And our house is kind of..." *Weird. Fucking crazy. Sentient?* "…quirky." Loney was staring at her, in a non-adoring type way. Confused. Wary? *Just say it!* "Well, I opened the box, 'cause it was supposed to fix the house, but Ed was trying to calm the house down, 'cause he can kind of talk to it, I guess you would say. The house calmed down, but Ed isn't Ed anymore, and he got on his bike and went to the graveyard and is just sitting there. In the grass. Above the dead people." She sighed.

Loney was facing the ground, frowning, looking at one thing, then something else. His eyes were darting back and forth, from underneath the bed, to the carpet, to a comforter, to something on the wall. It wasn't the same as his discomfort before; it was as if something she said had reminded him of something, but he couldn't quite remember what it was. Then it hit him.

"Whoa... is the box black and all kinda..." He made a strange shape with his fingers. "...shaped weird?"

"Yes!"

"Whoa...it's a scarebox!" Loney was getting really excited. Breathing quickly and walking back and forth. His nervousness was completely gone. This was something else.

"Yeah!"

"OK... whoa, man... this is—" Loney stopped and took a big breath. "Alright...sorry, I'm not usually like this, so jumpy and erratic, I'm just...Wait..." he stopped and looked at Od. "This is real, right? This is true? You're not... I mean, my brothers didn't have you say this?"

"I swear on the sword of my father, Domingo Montoya," Od said in all seriousness.

A genuine smile slowly crested then broke across Loney's face, and he immediately began digging under one of the beds. "I think Ed is basically just a body now." He pulled out some boxes, a wad of clothes, several magazines, and crawled under the bed further. Od could hear him mumbling something as he went but she couldn't understand him. When he emerged he held a wooden box.

"What'd you say?" Od asked.

He started again, but she found it really hard to listen to him with a pair of his underwear stuck to the box. Swinging back and forth as he talked.

"What?" Loney asked. Od made a face and raised her eyebrow at the hanging underwear.

Loney looked down, grabbed it, and threw it behind one of the beds.

There was an awkward silence.

The box was bigger, and browner, but kind of looked like... "Is *that* a scarebox?"

"No, listen. Ed's soul was scared out of his body." He started opening the box.

"Ed's soul was *scared* out of his body? What the hell does that mean?"

"Yeah, I know it's weird. There's these books that my mom and dad had—er—made, and a bunch of them are about different houses... I kind of thought that they were about hypothetical houses, or something, but I ALSO kind of secretly thought that they were about different houses here in town." Loney opened the wooden box. "Jeez.. my mind is blowing up right now. Seriously." In the box were comic books, all bagged and boarded just like Ed's weren't. He rifled through them.

"So, should I ask your parents about this? Can they help get Ed back or what?"

"I wouldn't ask them... Dad's gone... and Mom, well," Loney rolled his eyes. "Not a stellar idea."

"Fuck that. I need Ed back. Where's your mom?"

"No, Odlyn..." He looked her dead in her eyes. When Od looked into somebody's eyes that close, in some small way it changed how she saw them. "You have to get Ed's soul back into his body. Once he popped out he probably drifted into the house's...*other*... and maybe into, like, a pocket between worlds. In the pocket they don't see things the same as we do. For you to be able to communicate with him and for him to be able to get back into his body, he has to get out of the pocket and into the actual house. And to be honest, most of the time souls don't want to do that.

"Apparently it is really difficult for new bodiless to come back into our world. They get stuck. It takes them a long time to get out and do anything. By then they often forget about their old lives. Most of them, anyway. I think this is why a lot of them get hopeless and do weird, creepy things. But ghosts, or whatever they are, don't usually have their living bodies around by the time they get out of the pockets, so maybe his body will lure him out. What you need to do is bring his body back to the house. Then maybe his soul could be drawn to it—it doesn't really say that in the book, but I think it might work, especially since it's still alive."

"How could that be?"

"Huh?" Loney had been spinning a web of ideas, grabbing things he must have learned from the books and weaving them with Od's problem. It was interesting to watch.

"How is his body still alive and talking and stuff without his soul?"

"Oh…" Loney looked down, wrinkling his forehead for a bit, and then said, "I don't know."

"How do you know about all that other crap?"

"Guesses and books." Loney pulled one out. "This one." He held up the comic. A scary-looking house adorned the cover. It kind of looked like her house if it had been drawn by Bernie Wrightson. The title read *House N* in big, horror-themed typography. "And this one." He held up another with a wicked black box on the cover. Illustrated ghosts flew out of it, screaming into the night, and *Scarebox* was scrawled across the cover in blue ghastly letters.

"You read all of this in comic books? You learned this from *comic* books??"

"Yeah. My dad wrote 'em. My mom drew the pictures…I think. The story seems to change on who did what. Anyway, they know this kind of stuff."

"What? How? Why comic books?"

"Maybe because illustrations could explain better than just words. I don't know, really…because they're weird, I guess."

Od accepted that. She was weird, too. Sometimes that was the best way to describe something that would take a long time to explain, especially when you'd usually end up being misunderstood anyway. So, she let it go and fixated on what she needed to do.

"How do I get his *body* back to the house, then?"

"Hmm." Loney thought for a second. "I think you have to find something he wants, like ice cream or something. And dangle it in front of him. The comics don't go into huge detail about all the possible side effects of using a scarebox, but they did have one panel that mentions possible soulless bodies." Lonely flipped through the comic. "I don't think it's very common that they walk around, but it looked like you could put the soul back in..."

"So, step one: get Ed's body back to the house. With ice cream."

"No. Something he loves. Does he *really* love ice cream?"

"Doesn't everyone?"

"Yeah, but it has to be something he really, *really* loves. Like one of his *dreams*." Loney looked up and squinted, as if he was getting another idea. "Maybe he's in the graveyard 'cause he's drawn to other empty bodies—where they 'live' and where they belong." Loney continued to stare into space as he thought. "So...he feels like he belongs in the graveyard..."

"Dreams? Like wanting to be an astronaut or something? Or dreams like when you sleep?"

"What? No. One of the books said that some dreams stay in the body for a certain amount of time after the soul leaves." Loney stopped and tilted his head as if he had never considered the other meanings of the word before. "Hmm. I thought it meant the things that you love...Now that I say it out loud, it doesn't seem right."

"You have a bike?"

"Why...? Oh." Loney looked down at his hands, picking at his nails. "I can't go with you to the graveyard."

"Why? I thought Scrobes could do whatever they wanted."

"Yeah, right," Loney laughed. Then frowned a little in thought. "Well, I guess to some extent we can. But there are some things that each of us can't do no matter what. *I* can't go to the graveyard. Corlan can't... well, you get it. My mom can smell it on me if I go." Od stared at him. "What?"

"Do you really think that she can smell the graveyard on you?"

"Yeah." He wasn't going to go, and she needed him. He knew things, or thought he did anyway, and sometimes that was as important as knowing. Plus, she didn't have anybody else.

Od didn't really think about what she said next. Her brain just came up with the quickest way to get him to help her. And her mouth spit it out.

"I'll kiss you."

Loney looked at her lips. She didn't do it on purpose, but she licked them in the moment that he looked. She tasted Vanilla Lip Smackers. She saw him turn red and hoped her face getting hot didn't mean she was too. He still looked like he was weighing the options though.

"On the lips."

9

THE ARE

FOCUS. Ed wasn't sure if it was a voice or his mind. He tried to walk into the hallway, stomp-floating his way through the kitchen. As he moved through the doorway though, he found himself in the sunken living room again. The doll corner was quieter, but still alive. Ed tried to back away, up the step to the entryway, but it was as if the room was tilted, as though the floor slanted into the doll corner.

He slipped toward it and it awoke.

Focus. He tried to obey the word. But it wasn't working. There was no focus. The room was a cloudy slop of gray. *Focus or you will slip into the Pale. Use the tunnels, not the doors.* Ed could see things getting more vague: the piano became an oblong clump, propped with skinny clouded poles; the console stereo a rectangle block of ashen fog. He was slipping past the smaller, flowery blue couch, trying to stomp-float toward the big windows and the piano, but the room was tilting more. The Pale was slipping in. And he was sliding toward the doll corner. *Focus.* Ed focused. On being. On focusing. He focused tight and the pale gray of the room melted away as he did. The fireplace and hearthstone bench emerged from the blanched heather. The dolls in the corner were becoming not just a moving legion, but individuals. He was still sliding toward it though, and the dolls were beginning to notice him. One by one their tiny heads swiveled. The plastic eyes, made to spin in their sockets to appear more lifelike in the living world, rolled to find him. The ones with painted-on eyes moved their whole bodies. Still he slid.

He was a foot from the towering doll-case and they were all looking at him. From above. From below. From the sides. All of their little faces and eyes stared, waiting for him to get a little closer. He could not help but to oblige and slide…and they leapt for him. One jumped from a low ledge onto his leg. It grabbed fast and held on, climbing up him quick, squeezing its tiny doll fingers into his skin—*was it skin anymore?*—as it went. Two jumped down from the top shelf onto his chest and right shoulder. One from the center followed and another from behind that one, as if it had been waiting in line. More came. Jumping. Grabbing. Reaching in with their vicious little hands. Scrambling up or down him. Pinching with tiny digits. Biting with small mouths. They scraped at his chest, burrowed into his crotch, and dug at his ribs. They mumbled in raspy squeaks as they worked, the sounds orbiting him and permeating his being. Ed tried to pull them off, but he was so clumsy in this new world…and there were so many of them. The ones who could not find purchase in his front climbed onto his back and around to his backside, digging into his asshole. They were trying to tear into him wherever they could. They wanted to get *inside*.

Ed whipped back and forth, pulling dolls from out of his ass, and his crotch, but there were too many, and the ones he managed to pull away were just replaced with more. In desperation he flung himself before the fireplace, still resisting that slide toward the corner. It was cold and unlit, but it was further away, and maybe…as the dolls hooked into his soul he could feel himself sink into the floor. With every option he could see gone, he finally screamed. The dolls on his chest looked up at the sound and climbed his neck. They hooked their miniature hands into his mouth, pushing his scream back down. A red-haired doll with painted-on eyes clawed at his tongue and squirmed toward his throat. Others bore into his bellybutton and under his balls. He gave up resisting the tilt. They were getting in.

And then Ed was yanked, suddenly and violently, out of the house. Right through the wall with the fireplace in it. The dolls were forced to let go as a blinding light crushed him and set him spinning. There were trees and something else. The sun, maybe. Sky. Gravel. Pavement. Then he broke through another wall. Slapped onto a floor. More of the Pale. *Focus.* He tried to focus. The Pale dripped away a bit. He was in a long room with hardwood floors, strange posters on the walls. He could still feel the tilt. It slid him down the long room, touring the posters. One was of a sickly green man with a long mustache that turned into a river. A naked unattractive woman floated in that mustache river and something dripped out of her as she did. One was of a guitar filled with blood. One was of dozens and dozens of dogs all staring out at him with a forest to their right and a green star in the dark sky. Ed slid out of the long room and down four wooden steps, into an open kitchen with strange spaces, and then he was in a living room with painted red windows on all sides. A windmill music box sat on a mantle and played "Windmills of My Mind" in metallic tinkles. Still he slid.

Ed was dragged through what he assumed to be eight different houses, all bereft of people, none of which he recognized. Although he lost his focus after the first three, so they were masked in the Pale. He finally landed in a church. There was still a pull, but it must have been like a rubber band, where the resistance was greater the further away he was, because here it wasn't strong enough to rip him from the building. Which probably meant that he was close to whatever was pulling at him. The thought seemed backward to him…but also correct. He dug in against the weak tilt, not wanting to find out what was pulling him.

He had gone to preschool at this church. There was a big empty room at the center of the building where they would hold all their get-togethers, banquets, and receptions. It was technically a gymnasium, but he'd never seen it serve that purpose, and he didn't think of it as one, even though this was where they would have recess. During those recesses all the kids would scramble for the Big Wheels that were locked up in a room on the south side. The ones not lucky or fast enough to get one would have to settle for a simple tricycle, making up a game of their own, or playing with the old toy kitchen. Now it was empty. No toys. No kids. No Grandma Dorothy. He smiled at the thought of her, the patient and kind old woman who had worked there. Ed loved Grandma Dorothy.

This church was empty of the *things* in his house: no living dolls, no flame girls, no cats with black eyes, no mirror windows, but there was something there, in the building somewhere. He could feel it. It was in the chapel.

Ed stomp-floated into the chapel. He was getting better at it, but the constant pull didn't help. It was a decently sized chapel, mostly wood, stained but unpainted, with long stained glass windows and high wooden pews. The ceiling was non-existent in this version of the world, causing the walls to stretch upwards forever, fading eventually into a dark oblivion. The dais was raised in different sections, the tallest of which held an immense wooden cross that radiated in oranges, reds, blues, browns, yellows, greens, and grays. Not much of the Pale clung here, and Ed wondered if it had to do with the creatures at the center of the stage.

They were huddled in a circle at the front of the church, all of their arms—if they were arms—connected with one another, twisting and melting into each other, making it hard to tell where one began and another ended. None of them had much of a defined shape, just the general idea of a human—if a human had been a rock tossed in the sea and smoothed out on all sides for a millennium or three, that is. They might have been souls, or ghosts of some sort, or maybe something else Ed hadn't yet learned about or encountered when he was living, but the more he looked at them the more he became unsure of whether they had ever lived in the world Ed had grown up in.

As Ed came in, one of the things broke from the group and swam to him. It moved slowly and purposefully and as it got closer he could make out two holes in the front of it. The holes were the wrong size for eyes, and not quite in the right places, but he could sense sight from them. A couple more tore from the circle, swimming invisible currents that led to him, staring with holes of their own. More followed, breaking away from holding each other and drifting to him, floating down the aisles, through pews, and around the sides of the building. All of their looking-holes filled up with dull lights, some with reds or oranges, others grays or greens, more still with colors so faint he couldn't put a name to them right away. Some had only one looking-hole, others three or four, and there was one with five, scattered about its vague idea of a head like pips on a melted six-sided die. The holes were never quite in the correct spot for a living creature's eyes, almost as if the things had just heard rumors of where an eye should be, and that rumor had been passed down for a hundred generations, and now they each had their own interpretation of where they should be.

The things encircled him, their looking-holes lighting and dimming around him in an unsynchronized, yet deliberate fire-glow. If he had decided to run, there was nowhere to go.

Then one of the things with a single eye-hole floated towards him, its green hole burning, close enough to lick. *Somebody used to use that phrase, who was it?* Ed stared into the hole…and it whispered to him. "Young one. Born tonight. Welcome to The Congregation of the Cross. You're still tied to the waking world. Come fall asleep with us and start your Dream." The green light was so far inside of the thing. It stretched deep and endless. The words it said dripped from it, and he found himself wanting to fall into them.

"Who are you?" Ed asked. All of a sudden, he had found his voice.

The things whispered to him, "We are the sleeping world, we are the ones who hang onto the dream, we are the ones who are still alive. We are the resisters. We are the defiers of the dark. We are the fighters of the light. We are. We still are, as so many are not. We hold on."

"What?"

"Everyone gets the light and the dark choice. We choose neither, as neither is a choice."

And Ed knew what they were talking about. In the house he had seen the bright light of the front door and the darker-than-black void in the hallway. He knew he could go into them, but even when they beckoned him, he didn't want to go. It didn't seem right.

"So you choose to be ghosts?"

"We *are*. When you choose bright or night, you lose. You become nothing. You exist no more. We choose to be. We do not want to not be."

"Those aren't the doors to Heaven and Hell?"

"No. They are the choices of being erased or being consumed. Didn't you hear the voice?"

He did hear the voice. The voice that told him to focus. The voice that said to use the tunnels but not to use the doors. The light or the dark. Neither, it told him. Could it be? That this was the choice in dying?

"Who are you, though?"

"We are the Are."

"But individually, who are each of you? You don't even look like people. Maybe you're demons."

"This is the only life after the waking world. We have faded as we have been here. Our faces and bodies have become smooth. But you can see who we are in our mouths. The light of our lives still shines there." As the Are spoke, their mouths hung open in large slack shapes inconsistent with human mouths. Dull echoes of the light in their eyes shone there, where their words found another cavity from which to escape.

"What's with the cross?"

One with a brown light moved toward Ed. Its mouth hung crooked, long, and misplaced, dribbling light into the air along with its words. "We tie them to the cross." Another one with three yellow eyes came forward. A small mouth a bit too high on its face opened up and words fell out of it in a high-pitched rasp. "We save them." Another one came forward, one with orange eyes. A mouth opened up on its chest, way too large. A brighter orange light burst from it. "We built the nets and set them in the doors of the sick place. The young ones, the old ones, the weak ones all drift to the doors without choice. We catch them and save them. We peel strings off them and tie them up there. So that the doors don't eat them. The doors don't give them a choice, so we save them from being erased, save them from being consumed, we make them Are. They deserve to sleep, not to be no more."

"What the fuck?! Those doors are to Heaven and Hell! They probably have loved ones on the other sides, waiting for them. You are holding them prisoner."

"You are young. We are old. We know. You think you know, but the waking world knows nothing of sleep. There is no more after this. Better to be Are, than to be nothing. Being Are is living in sleep. Living all."

"How do you know that you get erased?"

"We know," a small gray light said.

"How?"

"We are old," a yellow light said.

"That doesn't mean anything. You can't even talk right."

"We don't usually…*talk*. We link and are Are. It is good. Nothing is not." A blue light.

"You aren't giving them a choice."

"The doors aren't. That is why we helped them." A pink light. Large. Soft.

"Fuck this," Ed said and stomp-floated toward the cross. Down the center aisle. Up the steps. He was moving better; it wasn't even much of an effort now.

"You are wrong. They should *be*." The single green light.

As Ed got closer to the cross, the lights upon it became more vivid. There were so many more of them than he had thought. Groans and murmurs in a hundred different voices pealed from the glowing cross. Mouths opened and closed. Eyes swam up and down. Hands. Bits and body parts. Fingers. An ear. All of it was running together, just like the lights were. Ed got closer. He could see the—thin, flat and transparent—that the Are had tied them with, binding the colors below.

"You don't know. You don't know. You don't know. You don't know. You don't know," the things told him. "It is bad." Green. Blue. Turquoise. Magenta. Lapis lazuli.

But he grabbed one of the transparent—more a strap than a string, really—and tugged. It bent outward, stretching. He grabbed it with both hands and pulled it apart until it snapped. A yellow soul split from the cross, sighed, and made a little moan as it tried to breathe. Gasps. More moans. It floated away, so small, and far too skinny, but it had more of a person shape to it than the Are. It had general facial features. Fingers. A vague outline of plasm around it. A white light opened before it in the wall behind the dais.

"No. no. no. no. no. no. no. no. no." The things were all around him now, all of their colors yelling at him.

The little soul touched the light and it began to steam and shake. Its mouth opened and a sound came out…a sound like screaming. It was halfway into the light now and it was frying—sizzling in the light, screaming louder and louder in a wondrous high vibration. Ed reached for it, stomp-floated for it, grabbed at it but missed, then realized he couldn't touch it without the clear strap, so he wrapped it around the soul and pulled. A quarter of it came out, just a partial head and a thin rope of body now, flopping and choking in the air. The other part had burned away. It twitched and its lone eye tore around the church. Then it stopped. It twitched once more, as if it had muscles and a bit of electricity still left in it, but that was it. It shriveled into the size of a quarter and hardened, then was swallowed by the Pale.

The Are looked into Ed. Their eyes grew wider, the colors deeper. Ed felt something close in around him. He looked down to see those clear straps tying his arms and his legs, dragging him upward to the cross, up to the other souls that were all tied together. A sharp twinge of panic rose past the general apathy that challenged him in this world. He felt himself wrap around the other souls tied to the cross and the panic melted for some reason. He drifted into them.

10

JASON

THE SUN WAS LEAVING, setting in the hills past the field they were playing in. Thin reeds sprang from the earth that grew sparser as the marsh crept in. The hunt was for the ball. They only had the one and they didn't want to go back to hitting rocks, especially since Bill had just gotten a real baseball bat for his birthday and didn't want to mess it up. Ed could understand that. Heck, he envied him for the thing. George spent about five minutes on trying to find the ball and had now abandoned the search completely and was hunting frogs, even though he was the one who had actually hit it into the muck and lost it. Now, since Bill was birdwatching or something, Harry and Ed were the only ones really looking for the ball, after all it *was* Ed's...*Wait, "Ed?" why did I just think of myself as "Ed"?* thought Jason. "Weird," he said out loud.

"What?" said Bill.

"Nothing." Jason frowned.

"A-ha!" George said from about twenty feet away.

"You found it!" said Harry.

"Nah." George came striding over, his feet covered in mud to the ankles. "I've got something better." He beamed with pride and thrust his prize out, dripping with mud.

"A frog?"

"Yeah, a frog," said George turning it over in his hands,

looking underneath it and at its tiny frog butt. "Hey Harry, you got any more firecrackers?"

"Of course. I got a whole thing of 'em."

"Let's fill his little green butt full of 'em."

"Let's find my ball." Jason was sick of George. He was always derailing a good game to do something stupid.

"It's goooone, Four-Eyes. We can try to come back again on Monday to try and find it, but there's no use looking right now 'cause I hit that thing into next week," George said. He thought he was clever and funny. In reality he was just a jerk.

"It doesn't matter how far it went—it was a foul ball," Harry said. He was their unofficial umpire. He still played, of course, but he made the best calls no matter whose team he was on.

"No way. That was a home run!" George cried. He shook his head as if to say that Harry was the idiot. "Anyway, who cares! If we can't find it, we can use the frog."

"That's a toad," said Harry.

"Use the frog as the ball?" Bill asked. He was obviously doubtful of how the game would work with a frog as a substitute for a baseball.

"Yes!" George said, as if just realizing what he himself had just insinuated.

"No way. I just got this bat—I'm not going to let you ruin it with frog guts," said Bill.

"Toad guts," Harry corrected.

"He couldn't even hit it, anyway. He swings the bat like a girl," said Jason.

"No, no, like my auntie!" Bill laughed. Nobody else did. Bill's auntie was in a wheelchair and had one good hand. It was a pretty good rib, but he had made fun of his own auntie in the process.

"Right. Pshhhhh," George said sarcastically. "That's why we

can't find the ball that I just murdered."

"You hit it into foul territory. That's why we can't find it, smart guy."

George looked at the frog, or toad, or whatever it was, then up at Jason.

"Hey, I bet you a nickel you wouldn't put it in your mouth."

"The frog?" said Jason.

"Yes."

"Why would I even want to do that?"

"'Cause you need a new ball." George sized Jason up. "And I'll give you a *dime* if you do."

"You're a loony," said Jason.

"And *yoouuuu* are a sissy," said George.

"Sissy!" somebody laughed out.

"It's just a frog. Worried your tongue's gonna get warts? Or worried it'll fall out and ruin the ladies' underwear you're wearing?" He couldn't get warts from it, could he? He decided to up the ante. If he was going to do it, he wanted some real money.

"A quarter," Jason countered.

"Deal!"

Jason and George both spit on their hands and shook.

"Five seconds in your mouth. I count."

"Lemme see the quarter."

George pulled the quarter out.

"OK." Jason grabbed the frog from George, who was bouncing up and down on his toes and trying to contain a smile. Only a jerk would take so much pleasure in seeing someone suck a frog. Jason looked the thing in the eyes and swallowed. *Better now than when it's in my mouth.* He opened his mouth and shoved it in, butt-first. It took up the whole of his mouth and just sat there, its frog head half in and half out of his mouth. The other boys were all laughing and saying 'ewwww' and making faces. Jason would have too, if he were one of them. It tasted like mud and bitter.

"One..." George was definitely taking his time.

"Two..." He was enjoying the whole thing. A big smile taking up half of his stupid face. Jason was beginning to think that George had lost the ball on purpose and engineered the whole thing to make somebody else miserable for five ridiculously long seconds, but that wasn't possible—George was usually crap at hitting, and wouldn't be able to target the marsh on purpose if his life depended on it.

"Three..." as soon as the number left his lips, George slammed his hand underneath Jason's chin and Jason bit into and through the frog, filling his mouth with guts. The thing twisted around violently as Jason tried to scrape it all out. He couldn't help the tears welling up as he watched it flop in the dirt. He had swallowed a bit of something but didn't know what it had been. That something had been washed down with a blood and piss cocktail squirting out of the creature's body and down the back of his throat. He started spitting and gagging, wiping blood from his mouth. George was laughing, hard. The others were making some type of noise, but he couldn't tell what, it was just one mash of sound. The frog was writhing on the ground with its innards sprawled in the dirt. It was wheeling around as if it thought it was still alive and could jump. Jason started bawling. He turned and ran toward home as fast as he could, stopping only once to rinse his mouth out with some water from a puddle.

As soon as he got home Jason ran right to his father. Still bawling. He told him about the baseball and the frog and what George had done to him. He cried the whole time. Then his father told him, "Go down to George's house right now. When you see him, you beat him until he cries as much as you have." His father said it calmly, although Jason could hear a tiny bit of anger on the outsides. "If you don't, I'm going to beat the living tar out of *you*."

Jason walked the half-mile to where George lived. He knocked on the door and asked politely to see him. When George came out, with a smile on his face that proved the pride he felt at doing such a nasty thing, Jason did it. He hit him. He had never hit anyone before, hadn't even squashed a bug bigger than an ant, never slapped somebody or gave them a dead leg, but he hit George square in the face. George stumbled back and Jason went after him, holding his fists as tight as they would go—so tight that they shook and turned color. George was dumbfounded. Just staring. So Jason got as close as he could and hit him again. He clipped his jaw. He swung again, with his left fist this time. It connected to the side of George's head and he went down. Jason wasn't thinking. If he started thinking he would start doubting. If he was doubting, he would stop fighting. He just kept hitting. He hit George's nose, and then his eye and then he missed his other eye and hit him in the forehead, then he hit him in the mouth and felt George's teeth open the skin on his knuckles. Then Jason stopped. It wasn't until then that George started wailing. Jason just sat there, straddling George around his stomach, and watching him bawl and bleed. He was dimly aware of his wrist beginning to hurt, but other than that he felt nothing inside. It was as if he wasn't even there. Then he was vaguely aware of being pulled away. George's mother was holding her son and ushering him into the house, throwing mean looks at Jason through her son's tears. Jason looked at the ground. Half buried in the loose dirt at his feet was one dull quarter...the next thing Jason was aware of was running down the dirt road that led to his house.

Jason's dad gave him a big slice of cobbler *with* ice cream. The cobbler was peach, burnt a little on the outsides, but still good...

...there were pale colors moving. Jason...no...*Ed* was drifting...he was himself, but he was also everyone else. Every soul tied together. Each one was a pool that you were connected to…part of…that you could fall into…one of them seemed brighter, or familiar maybe…or…no he was looking at himself…he *was* the pool…and he fell once more…

…TREES WHIPPED by the car window. Behind the trees on one side of the road, mountains. Behind the trees on the other side of the road, a cliff. Below the cliff was a lake. Ed watched the dappling of shadows on the pavement as they drove. Each time the car was in the sun he would clench his teeth together. Each time a shadow came he would un-clench. He imagined it as jumping over the shadows. If the shadow was on a certain side of the car and not the other, he would mirror it in his mouth. Left side sunny, right side shadow—left side teeth clenched, right side unclenched. It would get more difficult the more dappled the road became and the faster they went. The game sucked, but it kept the boredom at bay.

They were going into the city. Not a big city like Ellay or Sand Francisco, but bigger than the little town they lived in. It took about an hour to get there, and about seven miles from the city they crossed the Breathing Bridge. If he could hold his breath the whole way across it, his dad said he would get a wish. He had only gotten one wish that way so far, and he wasted that one. This time he gave it a dang good try, but about two sections from the end he had to take a breath. If it wasn't for that stupid RV in front of them he would have made it.

A few miles after the bridge were The Water Slides. It wasn't a water park really, so far as Ed could tell, it was just three tubes on the side of a mountain. Inside the mountain, really. All that was visible of the Slides from the freeway were the ends of them and the pool below that they emptied into. Ed had never seen anyone in there before and he thought that they must have had weird business hours. Not that he cared. Ed hated water parks and water slides. What if you got stuck inside? And *in* that hill! There would be no way to get you out. And you'd have all this water coming at you the whole time, going up your nose and in your ears and mouth. Lots of water was dangerous.

The Dannoven House was just outside of Reddville, down a road past all the antique shoppes and behind a few hills Ed had never seen before. It was an old Victorian-style house. Big. Pointy. With frivolous flourishes, a bit of stained glass, and porch that wrapped halfway around it. His parents had told him about this place, but he had never been there in person. Apparently inside were a bunch of kids that didn't have parents...and Ed was supposed to go inside and pick out a little brother.

Ed's perspective shifted...it went somewhere foreign, but familiar.

11

THE DANNOVEN HOUSE

AT NIGHT, WHEN OD GAVE UP ON finding faces in the ceiling dots, and of telling herself stories about the improbabilities of tomorrow, she would sneak downstairs and watch movies. The Dannovens had a bookcase in the front room filled, floor to ceiling, with videotapes, each crammed full of movies. Most of them were taped off of television or copied from rentals, filed in no particular order, except that the higher they were on the bookcase, the scarier the movies got. She started with the bottom row, with tapes that had titles like *Pete's Dragon*, *The Sword and the Stone*, *Babes in Toyland*, *Darby O'Gill and the Little People*, *The Shaggy Dog*, and *The Parent Trap* scrawled on their spines in three different colored pens—sometimes in cursive, sometimes in block letters. Movies like *Escape to Witch Mountain*, *Napoleon and Samantha, and Sammy the Way-Out Seal* became instant favorites. It was a labyrinth of cinema she'd get lost in each night, a comfort that she could close her eyes to. The sounds were married to pictures in her memories, and the cues would project the images on the inside of her eyelids. Those movies took root in her and colored the way she saw the world. They made her feel that if she was a good person, did good, helped those who needed helping, and sacrificed to help others, the world would be better, and everything would work out…somehow.

The comfort is what did her in, as always. She woke up one

morning to George Dannoven staring down at her. She had fallen asleep to *The Incredible Journey* and dreamed that she was lost with Luath, Bodger, and Tao, not sure if she had been a dog or a cat, or possibly some mix of the two. George was framed by the colors of the bookcase's videos and the backlight of the velveted window when he yelled at her. Static played in the background.

Od worked her way up the bookcase, finding *Willy Wonka and the Chocolate Factory*, *Superman II*, and *The Watcher in the Woods* on the ascent. Climbing higher, she discovered *The Shining*, *Jaws*, and *Dot and the Kangaroo* on the same tape, one that she'd return to many times. There were also Specials taped off of television; one with a creature named Salacious Crumb that showed how puppets were used and how they were operated, another was the Making of "Thriller", and there was a show all about science fiction movies. One image of a boy opening a front door with magic or aliens burning in amber before him conjured so many stories from her mind, both wondrous and terrifying. The higher tapes also had things like a video that was nothing but car chases, or gun fights, or lectures on how and why "the driver" shot JFK. One tape had *Invasion of the Body Snatchers*, *Night of the Living Dead*, and *Poltergeist* on it. It scared Od bad: that little girl with the spade, the sound of those pods opening, and Carol Ann looking into that television. They opened a new part of her that she hadn't known about before. She loved movies. She loved their images, and after watching them so many times—*The Black Stallion*, in particular—she fell deeply in love with their sounds.

After being locked in the closet for the fifth time, for watching movies when she was supposed to be sleeping, Od finally figured out how to become invisible. Strange enough, it was being locked in the closet that made her figure it out. All the kids at the Dannoven House called that closet the Ice Box, because it got unusually cold inside. Since Od spent a lot of time in there, she eventually found out why. There was a long, single A/C vent in there, behind a row of coats and shoes on the floor. She assumed it was there to keep the clothes cold on hot days. She used to put her head against that vent until it went numb, staring at the thin strip of light at the bottom of the door, and imagining it growing into a vast brightness. Beyond that brightness would be a field of snow and a family in snow gear waiting for her. It wouldn't be her own family, but they would be kind to her and let her build a snowman with them, and maybe they'd be back one day to take her home with them. After a few minutes she'd pull her head away from the vent and feel the coldness of her hair with her hands.

She was watching *The Dark Crystal* when she was thrown in the Ice Box for that fated fifth time. Margie Dannoven smacked her on the butt too, telling her that that movie was creepy and too scary for her, which Od thought was a thoroughly stupid remark. The smack startled Od, and the darkness took her by surprise when the door slammed shut behind her this time. It wasn't any darker than normal, but it hit her differently, and that sudden dark while still stuck in surprise made Od figure it out. All she needed to become invisible was Rachel Dannoven's red quilt.

Every night at nine the Dannovens would close the long velvet drapes in the parlor (as Margie Dannoven insisted it be called) and throw the TV and couch into black, just like the Ice Box. There was a red quilt that Rachel Dannoven kept in a trunk near the bay windows in the big living room, always folded very neat, in a perfect rectangle underneath this other random *thing* made of wood. Folding it in that perfect way after Od was done with it would be the hardest part. To become invisible she would just have to grab that red quilt and throw it over the top of the television. Then she would crawl under the quilt and get up real close to the tube, and turn the sound down to a "2". No light could dribble out and barely any sound could escape—not enough to travel into the hallway, anyway. She didn't test this as an outside observer, but she could feel it was true. It made her invisible. It made her part of the blackness. Sometimes it got too hot in there, but she loved it.

After doing this for a while, Od started to recognize when somebody was passing by, so she knew when to be extra quiet, to stifle her laughter at Danny Kaye hamming it up at the king's court, or her screams when the other Danny saw that hideous naked lady in room 237. She couldn't hear the people outside the red quilt as they passed, unless it was Britta or Parcel Dannoven, who clomped about as if they were a centaur, but she could sense them. It was The Girl who let her know when people were coming.

The people who ran the Dannoven House, the Dannovens, were nice. Kind of. They would sometimes bring ice cream and stuff on Sundays. And every Friday they would rent a couple of movies and order pizza. They would throw birthday parties for the kids on their birthdays too, with cake, although Od didn't enjoy the parties much. She didn't get along with most of the kids there except for Charlene, a girl—not *The* Girl—but *a* girl who liked fire.

Charlene was older by a few years. She always had candy and new toys, and she was deathly afraid of getting adopted. She told Od that if somebody adopted her that it would only be because of the money that her uncle had given to her. She had burns on the right side of her body from the car wreck that killed her family and she was fat from all the chocolate she hid, but she was cool. Her uncle lived on the coast somewhere with two girlfriends both of which had names starting with an "H." He didn't want Charlene. There was a rumor that he was afraid she would light his house on fire, like he thought she did to her family's car. Od didn't believe Charlene did that, and she thought that the uncle was a coward. Charlene ended up getting adopted by a man and woman with big puffy coats. It happened really fast, all in the same day. Charlene must have known before though, because she left Od a box full of candy and money. She also left her a My Little Pony with a shooting star on her butt. A note in the box said to keep it all secret, and Od did, except for the pony which ended up disappearing shortly after one of the Dannovens accused Od of stealing.

It was strange. Od never felt alone at the Dannoven House, even after Charlene left. Sure there were other kids that lived there, but that wasn't the reason—sometimes being around more people could make her feel more alone. It felt as if somebody was always with her. Another girl. *The* Girl, who was hiding and watching her that nobody knew about or could see. It was unsettling, but it was also nice sometimes, especially when she would think about all the mommies and daddies and brothers and sisters and grandmas, and great-great-grandpas that tell stories, and cousins who would take you for bike rides, and uncles who would sneak you into R-rated movies, and aunts who would scold the uncles for that, but who'd also sneak you candy, that she didn't have. When that sinking, sticky knowledge that nobody wanted her soaked through, and it did often, the Girl made her feel un-lonely. She knew the Girl couldn't keep her from the doom of the Dannoven House, though…and the doom was coming.

Od told Rachel Dannoven about the Girl. Rachel thought it was cute at first, but after a while she started squinting her eyes at Od. She looked at Od as if she were a snake, or a stain, especially when Od started telling her about getting feelings from other people. They would just ooze off them, pour into Od, and get tied up with her own feelings. To the point where she wasn't sure which feelings were hers and which feelings were those of the people around her. She stopped telling Rachel about the feelings when the older girl kept squinting, but by then it was too late; Rachel had told George and they both squinted at her. That was right about the time Od first felt the doom coming.

It was a vague doom. She didn't think it was the Countdown to Gone, as Jeremy called it. Jeremy was an older kid with big stupid teeth and tiny cruel eyes. He was always telling the other kids bad things, with his big stupid mouth. He would tell them about a man who would kill people because of when they were born. He said the guy would just go up to them in bright daylight and kill them, and the police had no idea who it was. He told Od once that every girl would be raped at least once in her life. He told a little kid that everybody gets in a car accident at least once in their life. That kid wouldn't ever ride in the car after that, and it cost him a foster parent. Jeremy also said that all the kids would be kicked out on their eighteenth birthday with no money and nowhere to go. The time that it took to get to that day was the Countdown to Gone. That wasn't what the doom was. The doom would be far before her 18th birthday.

As the months went by she could feel the doom getting closer. Inching each month. Then it was getting faster, eating up each week in big starving gulps. Finally she could feel it barreling down on her, screeching closer each day. Until Ed came in and picked her out.

That night, the night she left the Dannoven House and never went back, was the night a bathtub fell through the ceiling and crushed the television in the parlor. It fell at 1:03 A.M. Just when she would have been halfway through her second movie of the night. The doom feeling went away after that, and so did that strange, unsettling, comforting feeling of the Girl.

Something about the Scrobes reminded Od of the Dannoven House, though she couldn't point to a single thing that was similar. Something twitched in Od's thoughts about the mirrors in her hallway; they were like pools. *Od?...no, not Od...Ed* could see that there were things other than pools here tied to the cross with the others. And the pools were reflecting in each other and casting more pools...empty, reaching pools…tunnels. *Use the tunnels, not the doors.* The voice echoed again, in thought or memory. Ed fell against one of the pools in a thought. It was strange how physical wasn't even a thing now, just something far away—a bio-mechanical mess.

The tunnel rushed up to meet him, and he tumbled into his own bedroom.

PLAN Z

LONEY DIDN'T HAVE A BIKE, so he stole what Od thought must have been his brother's ten-speed. It was way too big for him and still had a baby seat attached to the back of it, so maybe it was one of his parent's, but either way he seemed to ride it as well as Od did the Mongoose. The ride back to the graveyard was silent. Embarrassment ate up most of the air between them, so there wasn't really any room for words anyway.

They had worked out the details of the kiss. It would be done at Od's house once Ed was back inside. On the mouth. For five seconds. No tongue. No hands anywhere. Just a straight-up on-the-lips black-and-white-movie kiss. They didn't specify whether they would close their eyes or not, but Od was thinking that she would keep hers open. It seemed more romantic when people closed their eyes to kiss and she did not want this to feel 'more romantic'. Although then he would be all close up and... Fine, it would be eyes closed and she could pretend he was Short Round, but then she might kiss him longer. OK, closed eyes, and she would pretend he was a frog. *I dare you to turn into a prince*, she thought.

Ed, or Ed's Body rather, was still sitting on the grass among some of the gravestones with a content little half-smile on its face. Od swung off the Mongoose and leaned it against a gravestone, making sure to read whose it was. It was only polite.

Ms. Madaline King
A Queen

"Ed."

Ed looked up at her and raised his eyebrows.

"You want to go watch some TV?"

He just stared.

"*Wonder Years* is coming on." Not a lie—it would be coming on, but not until Tuesday.

He blinked.

"We can rent a video. Like *Explorers*. Or some *Spectreman*?"

He turned to face a grave to his right, away from her.

Od reached into her backpack. There were only three things that she could think of that might make Ed disregard whatever attracted him to the graveyard. She pulled out a small rectangle, metal mostly, with black plastic, and rubber bits. The remote control to their family television. She presented it with her palms facing upwards, as if she were making an offering to a deity… or a horse. Ed looked at it and tilted his head. His pointer finger extended and flew low over it, buzzing the Enter Button and Numbers and stopped, hovering over the red On/Off. His finger lowered as if to press the button and Od pulled it back, biting the inside of her cheek, staring at her brother. He shifted forward, reaching out further. She took a crouching step backward, leading him away. He stopped, looked up at her and frowned. Then he went back to sitting. She moved forward again and held the remote in front of him. He smacked it out of her hand and turned away.

She reached into the bag again and pulled out a small man, rippling with muscles. A couple strips of armor crossed his chest and a mane of coifed yellow hair adorned his head. She tried to show it to him, but besides an initial cursory glance, he didn't look.

She laid it down and went for the last thing she had grabbed from their house to persuade him to move.

The golden cartridge wasn't just a faux-gilded piece of plastic, it was an adventure—a treasure that Ed had poured hours and hours into. Od had too, but it was technically his. He barely looked at it, even when she caught a stray light in its surface and bounced it into his eyes. He turned his back to her. She sighed and got up to get the remote. It was a little wet from the grass, so hopefully it still worked. She shoved it back into the bag after wiping it on her jeans and sleeved the game cartridge. She couldn't find the action figure.

Od turned to Loney, who had gotten off the big ten-speed and was now watching them from atop a weathered gravestone. "Nothing," she said.

Loney hopped down and stood in front of Ed. "Hey. Ed... er.. Yeah, I guess it's Ed, right? I mean, you're Ed's body, but there's obviously still some Ed in there." Od shook her head as Loney continued. "You wanna play *Ultima* or *Castlevania*, or *Tecmo Bowl*, maybe?" He didn't even turn towards Loney. "I have a bunch of comics you can have. Good ones." Ed didn't move. "I just got a bunch of Space set Legos. Haven't even opened them. You can have a couple if you want." Nothing. "We're leaving right now to go to Disneyland." Ed straightened up and began to turn toward Loney, but something overrode the action. He...or it...slumped back down and started playing with the grass.

OD AND LONEY SPENT the next hour and a half trying to figure out what could make Ed's Body come back to the house. Nothing got much of a reaction from it. It did say *something* at one point, but what it said didn't make any sense and it didn't even seem to be talking to either one of them when it said it.

"Now what?" Od said.

"Plan 9."

"Plan B, you mean?"

"Plan 9. Like from outer space… it's a movie… never mind." Od rolled her eyes. "OK then, Plan B." Loney cracked his fingers and his back and then lunged at Ed's Body. He grabbed it and wrapped his arms around its torso, trying as best as he could to drag it away from the graves. Ed's Body screamed, then punched Loney once in the shoulder and then in the stomach. Loney dropped to the ground. Ed's Body screamed once more for no reason and then sat back in the grass.

Loney was struggling to get the air back into his lungs. He was forcing himself to breathe through his nose for some reason. "*That* was Plan B?" Od asked, walking over to him. "What were you going to do, drag it all the way back to the house?"

Loney was out of breath. "I… don't... know..."

"Ed's got like fifty pounds on you."

"Well, I have one more idea... Plan Z."

"Why Z?"

Loney stood up and scanned the graveyard. "Instead of bringing his body to your house," he rubbed his shoulder and rolled it in its socket, "since that doesn't seem possible, let's bring Ed's soul here."

"Can we do that?"

"We just need something to put it in."

"Like…?"

Loney gestured to himself as if he was showing off a new suit. "Like a body."

Od frowned at him.

"I'm trying to work with what we have here."

"Like one of *our* bodies?!"

"No, no..." But what Od said made him pause for a second and think. "Hmmm..." Loney physically shook the idea away and went on, "No, I was talking about working with our *surroundings*." Loney spread his arms out again and then gestured to the graveyard, the stones, and grass. Loney was obviously trying to say something, but didn't actually want to say it out loud for some reason. Then Od got it.

"You're seriously mental."

"No, it should work. We just have to find a fresh enough corpse to be able to make it there and back again."

Od stared at him. "No."

"Yeah."

"Is this in your comic books?"

"No. But it is an *educated* guess." He was proud of it.

Odlyn laughed. "You want to desecrate somebody's recent grave, steal the corpse, walk it to my house, somehow coax my brother's soul into it, have him walk his rotten ass back here, and then transfer his soul back into his original body?"

"Yes." Loney smiled. No, he was beaming, like he just figured out how to turn dirt into diamonds. "But I was hoping that once in the, uh, surrogate body, he could ride a bike, that way we wouldn't have to put a leash on him or something. I mean, once you learn to ride a bike you never forget, right?"

"No way."

"Well, I can always go home and play Nintendo."

Bastard. "So this is it? This is the only plan left?"

"That's kind of what Plan Z refers to."

Od stopped to think a second. "But wasn't the whole point that his own body would lure his soul out of the pocket, especially since it was alive?"

"Yeah, but I bet another empty body could do it. We can tell him to go inside it. And since his body is still alive somewhere and his soul prolly knows it, maybe that would help?"

"How would we even get the body back to the house?"

"Hmmm..."

If his soul could go into another dead body, was it possible that another ghost could get into Ed's Body while he was in the graveyard? Od wondered. *Is it just an open invitation right now?* Ed's Body sat in the grass, looking at nothing, with no expression —just being.

13

THE GRAND NATIONAL

ODLYN KNEW EXACTLY WHERE the spare key to the Buick Grand National was, even though Bob had hidden *and* camouflaged it. He rarely drove it, just rubbed it with a diaper or whatever, and kept it in his garage like a trophy. The thing could go zero to sixty in less than five seconds and had the power of 245 horses. It was a black steel dragon. And dragons didn't want to stay in their caves—they wanted to fly, they wanted to eat, and they needed those things to survive. The Grand National was made to sail the streets, to consume the pavement—to live. And tonight it was going to.

The key was hidden in the fence that separated their property from Bob's, in a hollowed out piece of wood. Od had seen him put it there once while she was climbing on the roof of their garage. She hadn't known what it was while she was up there, but after she retrieved the stuck basketball that inspired the journey to the roof, and Bob had gone inside, she snuck over and found it. Why he kept it there she had guessed at, but didn't know the truth of. Not that it really mattered. What really mattered was that the side door to his garage was unlocked, as was the car itself, just like ninety percent of doors in their town.

She slid into the blackout interior of the powerful beast.

Thrust the key into the ignition and turned.

It thundered to life.

The garage was a good twenty yards from the main house, so hopefully Bob was a deep sleeper. She bit her lip and opened the main garage door, which was apparently the loudest thing on planet Earth, and took longer to rise than Das Boot did to finish. She rolled the Grand National into the driveway, keeping the lights off until she could hit the main road and pilot it into the night.

Od fit the Buick like she never did the Subaru Brat. Not that she didn't like the Brat, it just wasn't her. The Brat was her father though, everything about it. It was because of how he drove the Brat that made Od want to drive. How he took to the dirt roads, how he punched the gas, and his expressions when they were on a Saturday mission to the dump, put driving into her heart. She asked him to teach her and he had let her steer the thing a few times, but she wanted to *really* drive, and he said she was just a little too young for that. So she made it happen herself.

She taught herself by watching what her mom and dad did when they drove, memorizing their movements and timing. Then at night she would sneak out and try the pedals without turning the car on. After she got her courage up, she turned the engine on and tried the pedals for real, strapping boxes to her shoes like Short Round did in *The Temple of Doom*. The pedals were tricky, mainly because of the timing, but she had plenty of time to learn since she didn't have to swipe the keys each time. Her parents kept the spare key to the Brat in a drawer in her dad's workshop. It wasn't hidden to the extent that Bob's was, but it wasn't in the first place somebody would look for it either. Not that anyone would, save her of course.

At first she only took the Brat out on their driveway when nobody else was home, circling their house a couple goes at a time, but after watching her dad shift and step on the clutch a few dozen times, after she went through a book and two videotapes from the library, and after practicing with the engine off over and over again, she got the hang of shifting. It was different when the engine was running, and much more difficult, but soon she could feel when the engine needed something and when she should shift. She could hear it. After letting her steer for the first time her dad told her that she was a natural pilot, and she believed him. Belief could accomplish a lot.

After it became boring to drive around the house, and she was confident in shifting, she took to the back roads. She could drive the hell out of the Brat. She could tear up the Dirt Sea, the Timber Strait, and all the dirt backroads of Timber Hills, but the little truck didn't really fit her. The Grand National fit. It was like a muscle of hers now. A suit of armor. Or a robot she controlled from within. It *was* her. She pulled her foot off the gas and punched the clutch, shifted, and then slammed the accelerator. The Grand National wore the snaky mountain road like a leotard. Of course she still had to strap the boxes to her feet, which she had constructed out of dictionaries and duct tape, but they slipped on and off easily and they made her, in a way, whole. She called them her co-pilots.

Od picked Loney up down the street where she and Ed caught the bus for school. He buckled himself in right away and glued his eyes on the concrete before them. She didn't think he fully trusted her, which kind of made her want to take the turns at full speed.

In the sideview mirror, at the foot of the small hill that rose just behind the bus stop, bathed in the red of the brake lights, were several gopher holes.

"I need to know something," Od said.

"What?" Loney kept his eyes on the road.

"About the cats."

Loney didn't say anything.

"There's a rumor at school." Od stole a look at him to see his reaction. "About the holes in your yard… and cats."

Loney looked out the passenger window. *God, this is the*

wrong time to ask this, Od thought. *Don't ask him.*

"Loney!"

"What?" He yelled it.

"Is it true?"

Loney didn't say anything.

"Loney, is it true?"

"...kind of."

Od's eyes blurred with tears. "Get out—" she started, but she needed him. For Ed. She wouldn't be here, wouldn't be alive, if it weren't for Ed. Loney didn't budge. A rage built up in her chest, fueled by sadness, and...why did she feel betrayed?

"How much is true?"

"Which version did you hear?"

"That the cats were buried in the ground... up to their necks, with their heads sticking out of the dirt, and then... the lawnmower..." Od choked up.

"...mostly true." He wouldn't look at her.

She couldn't not look at him. How could a face like that do something so horrible? It was like a monster had tied a normal little boy's face on over its own. "What's not true?"

"They, uh... they weren't cats." Loney looked up at the sun visor above the windshield, then out at the street, then at the glovebox. "They were kittens," he said.

Od turned in the driver's seat and smashed her fist into Loney's head. His head bounced off of the passenger side window. Her wrist hurt immediately and it was tough for her to keep a fist, but she was crawling over the gear shift and, grabbing his shirt and hitting him again in that human face. That mask.

"Whoa!" Loney screamed. "What the hell?!" His hands were up in front of his face trying to block the hits. "It wasn't ME! I didn't do it!"

She was still hitting.

"I PROMISE! It wasn't me."

And then Od knew it like a lightning bolt. "It was Gatch."

"...yeah." Od could see a sort of battle within Loney. A reluctance. A loyalty?

"And you let him?"

"I don't *let* Gatch do anything. He does what he wants."

"He's eight!"

"So?"

"So you can stop him. He's small. Or you could tell your mom or brothers." But Od didn't really believe that would help.

"Gatch is a lot stronger than he looks. He's not awkward like other little kids. We can't stop him; he is the Will. Plus he has Corlan and Bray. They are his...nevermind. They look after him exactly how they don't look after me." Something was odd about how Loney said Will. Like it was capitalized. Important. "I wasn't there. When it happened. But mom said it was my fault, so I had to...clean it up."

"Why was it your fault?" Od couldn't help the images of *cleaning up* the kittens from creeping into her mind and nesting there. She physically shook her head, trying to shake the images away.

"'Cause I let Chimes get pregnant. She didn't listen to me, stupid cat. And a little cat came by one night and, well I thought he was a kitten, but he was full-grown, just little. And well, they uh... I don't know if you've ever heard cats doing it before. I don't think they like it as much as people do. Anyway, I scared him away once I realized what they were doing, but I guess it was too late. Mom said she was pregnant and it was my responsibility. I thought I was going to have to take care of the kittens or take them down to the market in a cardboard box and give them away. But no... Gatch killed them. And they all said it was my fault. So I had to clean it up."

"What. The. Fuck," Od said. "That isn't normal." She felt weird saying that. She'd never thrown that word around like that. Normal was something she had wished for, but could never find. People seemed to blame you for not being normal. Like it was a choice. Saying that something wasn't normal was such an unfair accusation, like blaming a kid for being poor or an orphan. "That wasn't your fault."

"I know," Loney said. "But I wanted to clean it up anyway. They would've just thrown them away. Or fed them to the dogs or something. I buried them. They deserved that. They were just babies."

Loney just sat there staring out the window into the dark. Od choked down the sourness in her throat, wiped her eyes, and drove.

14

DEVOTION

OD PARKED THE GRAND NATIONAL behind the community mausoleum in the back of the graveyard.

"So."

"So."

She killed the engine and turned the headlights off.

"I was thinking," Loney said. "The mausoleum is probably our best bet."

The mausoleum had two entrances; one in the front and one in the back, both with double doors made of glass surrounded by transom windows and sidelights. The front door was set under a simple colonnade that was void of decoration and the rest of the building's exterior was made up of three different shades of white brick that had been mismatched in a purposeful way. Above the front doors were brushed metal letters, spelling out a single word. *Devotion.*

An array of off-putting whites washed the entirety of the inside. Black and gold veins ran the walls, connecting the floor to a ceiling remarkable only for its skylights. During the day it felt like a neglected greenhouse, stifling and humid, smelling like old flowers, wet leaves, and disinfectant. The place was usually silent; only small personal sounds like shoes or whispers took residence there, and those produced tinny echoes, not what one would expect from its marbled appearance. Those sounds were sometimes livened by muffled bird chirps or lawnmowers, and occasionally tires on dirt, but now it was just a blank night sound—no crickets, no cars.

The walls were segregated in marble rectangles, some of which having little plaques that summed up a person's life in as few words and numbers as possible. The lucky ones had either a quote or sentiment of some sort. The quote wasn't something the person behind the plaque had ever said, and the sentiment didn't describe their lives in any way—they were something that whoever paid for the plaque picked out for them. They were all, in Od's opinion, unbearably generic. She read the dates on the plaques. *This is what they must mean by becoming a number*, Od thought. You couldn't tell if the people were fat or skinny, or what color eyes or hair they had, if they liked pizza, caviar, or ten-cent ramen, if they had saved somebody's life or had taken it from them. You didn't know if they ever hit a home run or stole home plate, starred in a film or destroyed a great piece of art, gave away their money or hoarded it until they died; they were all just another marble brick in the wall.

Od could feel the chill coming off the darkened marble surrounding them. She had been in there a few times before with her friend Katie, but it had almost always been in the daytime. Katie was really into stuff like graves, skeletons, mummies, and death… well, before she became a cheerleader anyway. Od was still deciding whether she was going to try and be a cheerleader or not next year. She wondered if any of the people surrounding her in the mausoleum had been cheerleaders and if they liked it or not. So many forgotten stories. So many dead thoughts that would never be expressed.

Loney had tried the left back door, but it was locked, so Od broke a tiny window on the side of the door, reached in and unlocked it. There was a flashlight in the back seat of the Buick, but they didn't really need it since the lights were always on in this dead place. They both set to scour the plaques for the most recent dates of death and after their tour they found a few plaques with dates from within the last few years. The names of the lucky contestants were: Acton Fields, Joseph Calder Winters, and Emily Cline.

"So, Acton or Joseph?" Od asked. "Acton is a boy's name, right?"

"Yeah. It's your call."

"Flip a coin?"

"Yeah, let's flip to see which corpse we steal." With how Loney said it, she wasn't sure if it was a joke or not. How could it not have been, though?

"We're not keeping it. We're going to bring it… *him* right back." Od got out a quarter. "OK, heads for Acton 'cause he has this halo thing on his plaque. Tails for Joe 'cause…he's the other one." Od flipped it into the air, caught it, and slapped it on the back of her hand. Tails. "Joe."

Od had found a pretty wicked-looking hammer in Bob's garage, along with some rope and a few other things that she threw into the back seat with the flashlight when she had boosted the car. Loney had the hammer now. He aimed at the marble next to the plaque. Swallowed. Pulled the hammer back and—

"Wait!" The little marble rectangle was *too* little. "Joe isn't in there. I mean, he is, but I think these are just his ashes. Look at how small it is." Loney let the hammer fall to his side. "What about Acton?"

"Nope, he's ashes too." Loney confirmed after walking over to Acton's small marble rectangle.

Emily Cline wasn't, though. She had a big marble slab in the other end of the mausoleum next to the other big marble slabs where they must have kept the full bodies. The most recently deceased full-bodied *guy* in the Devotion mausoleum was Henry Patrick Jordan and he had died five years ago. Loney looked at her. Od sighed and bit the inside of her cheek.

"Ed is going to kill me," Od said. "I use his soul to animate a corpse, probably the coolest thing to ever happen to him, and it has to be a girl." She shook her head.

"Wait! Since we have the car now, why don't we just go over there and force Ed's Body in the back seat? I already tried to tackle him earlier, but you and I could maybe do it together."

"If we get him in there he's going to be all crazy in the back or open the door and jump out while we're moving. We'd have to tie him up or something. And Duck Tape his mouth. Even then he might still thrash around and cause us to crash."

"Well, we can't put him in the trunk." They had looked in the trunk. It was full of random stuff. Bars and pipes and electronics were all attached to something bigger underneath. They didn't know what that bigger thing was, but they couldn't move it. It might have been attached to the bottom of the trunk somehow. If Ed had been a tiny bit smaller they *might* have been able to fit him in, but as it happened Ed was big for his age. "Maybe we could knock him out, like in the movies," Od suggested.

"I don't think that we wanna do that. A blow to the head that can knock a person unconscious is a hard enough blow to kill them. Even if it doesn't kill him, it could cause permanent brain damage and he could stay unconscious forever. Like a coma. Plus he doesn't have his soul in him—what if knocking him unconscious just knocks the last of bit of life out of him?"

"Every movie ever has been lying to me."

Loney chuckled. "Yeah...well at least really stretching probability."

"Hmm."

"So."

"OK, let's meet Emily Cline."

They used a big screwdriver powered by the wicked-looking hammer to break the seal around the marble slab, and after prying it from the wall let it drop to the floor with a loud crack. The casket fit loosely in the vault with what seemed like too much space around it. It looked lonely. Od bit the inside of her cheek. There was a woman's body in there. A dead woman. A once-alive woman. Od felt a tingle between her shoulder blades and looked behind herself. Ed's Body was standing outside the front double doors, staring in at them. It wasn't a look she had seen before.

"Ed!" Od whispered. She walked to the front of the mausoleum and unlocked the door, but Ed's Body just stood there staring at her. Staring at the coffin. "Come on." But it wouldn't move. It just stared. She went over to it and opened the door. "Get in here!" She grabbed its wrist and it pulled away with a yelp. "Fine!" Od shut the door but continued to steal looks back at it. Ed's Body continued to stare in.

They tied each end of the rope Od had found to the handles on the sides of the casket and then wrapped the excess around themselves and pulled. It was heavy, but not as heavy as they thought it would be. It fell to the ground, loud, and sudden. *Shouldn't it be much bigger?* She gasped. The metal inscription with Emily's name, birthday, and deathday, lay bent on the ground. It read:

Emily Cline
1979-1986
"Alone no more."

Od gasped. *Seven years old.* "She's a little girl," Od said.
"Oh, fuck…" Loney wiped his nose on the back of his hand.
"We already did it," Od said, looking at the tiny coffin. She

stood staring down at it for what might have been a minute or an hour. Then she spoke again. "This won't hurt her."

"Technically, yeah." Loney was staring at the coffin. "You think this will hurt her parents, though?"

What would Od do if someone opened the grave of somebody she loved, used the person and put them back? *Damn, how did I get here?* When you do something for the right reason, with just that something in mind and at the center of every decision, other things become blurry. The line between right and wrong keeps moving as you compare consequences and intentions of the moment, and the moment keeps moving. It might cause the girl's parents pain, but this girl's parents were adults. Adults could handle things in ways that kids couldn't; they were steeled, and their hearts weren't as delicate. In some ways adults were already dead, the children they were, the dreams they dreamt, the fears and pains they guarded. All of their color had been washed away and replaced with rhetoric and numbers. "Pain for a few adults to keep a kid alive is worth it."

Loney was looking down. "Pain can be worse than death."

"No. Death is forever."

"Not for Ed." Loney looked up at her.

"Ed's not dead."

"I know. He's still in your house."

"Yeah, maybe, hopefully… but for how long? Is he going somewhere after? Is he going to be trapped in the house forever? Is it holding on to him? What if he's just going to fade away? They call ghosts *fades* sometimes, right? What if he fades into not existing anymore? Or worse—what if he's trapped and suffering?" Od looked down at the little casket. "We already pulled her out of the wall. The pain will be the same no matter what we do now."

Loney was crouching next to Emily's casket. "Maybe she didn't have parents." He picked something up and rubbed it with his fingers. "Her plaque says, 'Alone no more'." He gently placed it back onto the ground and stood up again. "At least it will be easier to carry a little girl." Neither of those things made her feel any better, and she still wasn't sure if he was making a joke or not.

The lid of the coffin was white with a matte finish, and the outside of the casket was dry and dusty. *Thank goodness for that.* Od knew what happened to dead bodies in wet areas. Katie Cooper had read her all sorts of things against her will about dead bodies and what happened to them. Those things would be stuck in Od's brain for all eternity—fun.

There were words cut into the trim of the small death-box with an abundance of flourishes and curlicues and Od found herself tracing them with her mind, but not comprehending what they said.

They popped open the casket with the grave-key Katie had originally found a year or so before. It was in an unlocked lockbox near the back of the mausoleum then, and that is where Od found it now. Back when they were best friends, she and Katie would take the grave-key out to play with. It would always play some pivotal role in their game or hold some mysterious power. It would be a talisman or a weapon, or simply an artifact that held the answers to the questions they sought. Katie even showed Od how to use it, though how she obtained that knowledge Od could only guess at.

Ed's Body was still watching Od and Loney from behind the glass front door, arms at its side, eyes unblinking, with that unknown look on its face. When the lid popped, Od wished that she was outside with it.

The smell of death was *heavy*—that was the only way she could describe it—and it felt as if that smell was seeping into her clothes and hair. It smelled sticky and sick. Like vomit baked in the sun, or soaking garbage left fermenting for years, or diseased meat stuffed into bedsores…no, it just smelled like death, like *heavy*. She vomited on the floor. The sound of the puke hitting the marble made her retch again for whatever reason, and when she breathed through her nose because she was retching, she gagged on the smell again. It had a *sweetness* to it. But a bad sweet. A too-sweet. A sweetness that was trying to get into you, and would eventually. An ever *wrong* sweet. After she picked herself up from gagging at the floor she plugged her nose and covered her mouth. Loney was just finishing throwing up as well. He wiped his mouth with his sleeve.

"Oh... god." Loney gagged again. "I—" He got up and stumbled to the back door and out into the night. Od held her breath and pulled her shirt up to cover her nose and mouth. She grabbed the lid of Emily Cline's coffin and pulled it as hard as she could. It came up easily, letting loose an even thicker stench.

Emily Cline was even smaller than Od thought she'd be. She had dark hair and wore a green dress with a matching green ribbon around her neck. Thank goodness she had been well preserved. Her eyes had sunken back into their sockets though and black spots blossomed around them, almost connecting her missing upper lip to her deflated cheeks, but her dress was clean and her shoes were still shiny. They were cute, black Mary Janes.

THEY CARRIED EMILY CLINE from the mausoleum to the Grand National together, Loney holding her arms and Od her legs.

"She's not going in the trunk."

"What?" Loney squeaked. "Why?"

"Because she doesn't deserve that. She already had to die as a little girl."

"What if we get stopped by the cops?"

"If we get stopped by the cops, then we're screwed no matter what. Driving without a license. Grand Theft Auto." She thought she was using that term correctly. "Plus, I know she's a lot smaller than Ed's Body, but I still doubt there's enough room for her in there." She did doubt it, but it was a weak doubt.

"Yeah, so why add grave robbery, destruction of public property, and corpse-stealing to that?" Corpse-stealing didn't sound like a thing, but it had to be. *Who owned dead bodies? Was it the cemetery? Or was it the family, and they were just renting the space in the mausoleum? And if the family did own it, what about a body that didn't have a family, who owned it then?*

"If we get pulled over, they're not going to let us go, and they're going to find the body in the trunk. It's pointless and *rude* to put her in the trunk." Od dropped one of Emily's legs. "And she's wearing a seat belt." She flung the passenger door open.

THE DRIVE BACK to Od's house was fairly uneventful, but Loney found a mixtape in the door and put it on as the pulled out of the cemetery. The first song on the tape was "Girls Just Wanna Have Fun" by Cyndi Lauper.

THEY PARKED on the opposite side of Od's house, away from Bob's in case he woke up and happened to recognize the sound of the engine or decided to peek through the fence for some reason in the middle of the night. That didn't seem likely, but adults were strange creatures. Od forgot to put the outside lights on before she left, so she ran into the house and flicked them on, but then she decided it would be better to carry the dead girl in in the dark, no matter what they might trip over, so she flicked them off again.

Going back into the house felt wrong, like she shouldn't be there or like something was out of place, but she couldn't put her finger on why that was. It almost felt as if the house was watching her and didn't quite approve of what she was doing. She had felt that before a couple of times, the first of which being when she initially came to the house. Back then she thought that it was all in her head, that she was just feeling out of place and it was causing her to feel like she was being watched and judged by some unknown all-surrounding entity. But now she *knew* it was the house that was making her feel that way before, and that it could very well be watching her now. Watching was the wrong word. The feeling became slippery when she tried to analyze it and made her unsure. Maybe it was her emotions getting twisted up in the moment. After all, it wasn't thick or thin inside the house, just wrong. Maybe it was the absence of her dogs that was creating the feeling. She usually had to let Walt Disney and Steve Martin in once it got dark, but they were still out back, and they would have to stay out there for now. She wasn't sure how the dogs would react to a dead girl, and she didn't want to find out.

They set Emily in the spinning brown comfy chair just off the kitchen next to the wood burning stove. "OK, so how do we put him inside her?"

Loney chuckled for some reason.

"Does she need to, like, *be* in the room where he left his body?"

"No." Loney looked around the room. "I think Ed probably went to wherever the least amount of...uh...activity is."

"Like ghosts?"

"Yeah, kinda. Like, there's gotta be some weird stuff stuck in that pocket he's in. And..." He trailed off as he craned his neck to look into the den. "Do you guys have any dolls?"

"Guess you didn't look in the living room as we passed it?"

"Nope."

"My mom has hundreds of them."

"Oh man... And they're all in the living room?"

"Most of them. Why?"

"Ed's for sure not in that room."

"Why?"

"Souls and stiggs like dolls. They can live in them or get stuck in them. Also dolls can manifest strange things on the *other* side. To a recently bodiless, they would be kinda scary."

"Are they dangerous?"

"Probably. Not sure. There isn't much on inter-soul interaction in the books. I don't think my mom or dad had any direct experience with the...uh...*beyond*." It sounded as if Loney was trying out different words to call the place where the ghosts and *other* things were.

"So. What do we do?"

"Well, now it gets complicated. We have to find the left finger of two women. One of nineteen. And one of ninety. Once they are cut off and placed in a bowl of salt they will point to where Ed is."

"What?!"

Loney started laughing.

"You're joking? You suck."

Loney laughed again.

"It's not even funny." *It was* kinda *funny.* "So what do we really do?"

"Wait."

"Wait?"

"Yup."

"What's he gonna do, just go in the body? What if another soul goes into it? And what's a stigg?" That's what he said, right? *Stigg?*

"Hopefully he'll be able to feel us in the house, wherever he is. He'll come here, see the dead body and go into it? I don't know how well he can see people from where he is. Maybe he'll think the body is his? This all became theoretical a while back. A stigg is kinda like—"

"What if he doesn't? Can we let him know somehow that is

what he has to do?"

Loney shrugged, so Od went into every room and said out loud, "Ed, come to the kitchen." Maybe he could see and hear her, maybe not, but at least she was doing something; waiting felt like doing nothing.

THEY WAITED UNTIL 3:37 A.M. Around midnight Od found some Vick's VapoRub and they both smeared it under their nose to drown that death smell. Around 1:00 A.M. Od let Walt Disney and Steve Martin in since they were barking and scratching at the door nonstop. They had gotten into something while they had been outside because their paws were dirty to the ankles. Od noticed immediately since both dogs were mostly white—*ghost dogs*, her dad called them—but she ignored it. Od always thought Walt Disney looked as if she had run amuck through the Ink and Paint Department that she had read about in Burbank. She had spots in random places, all different shapes, sizes, and colors. It had made for a good excuse in the past for not knowing she was dirty, but that didn't really work with the other dog. They were both at least half Samoyed, but Steve Martin must have been part something else that was even bigger, because he was at least six inches taller than his counterpart. His fur was something everybody commented on since it was so unique. His head was completely white, but as you went down his body it faded in a smooth gradient to dark gray. His tail was black and his paws were all white.

Steve Martin growled at the body when he came in and Walt Disney looked like she wanted to eat Emily, so after she explained their names to Loney, she put them in the den and closed the accordion doors. Around 2:00 A.M. Od found an old Pizza Parlor box, tore off the lid, and wrote:

Ed.

Possess this girl.
We'll explain later.

She put the sign neatly on Emily's chest.

But he still didn't show up.

"So now what?"

"So now... I don't know."

"Consult the comics?"

"No. I know them by heart." Loney had his thinking face on again. He was tracing the floor with his eyes, then he let them run up the walls. "Hey, what's your phone number?"

"What?"

"Well…I don't know." He looked kind away.

Od didn't say anything. Were they friends now? Is that why he was asking? It obviously didn't have anything to do with their current problem. They were a lot closer to being friends than they were yesterday, at least. He had done more for her tonight than almost anyone she knew for the whole time that she knew them.

"It might be useful to know at some point," said Loney.

"3501." No need to say the first part, everyone in town had the same prefix. "Yours?"

"6136. But don't call it," said Loney.

Od smiled.

"No. Seriously. Don't call it." He looked like he was joking and serious at the same time.

"OK." Od said, "So what do we do now?"

"Wait more?"

"Can't we ask your mom?"

He looked her dead in the eyes. "Not a good idea."

"Wouldn't she know?"

"Maybe."

"Then let's ask her."

Loney shook his head emphatically and sighed. "I'm sure we can figure it out."

"Hey, my parents are coming back at 11:00 A.M. We need to figure this out. Not to mention it's going to be tomorrow soon and everyone in town is going to wake up and we still need to put Emily Cline back. AND we need to put the Grand National back." Then she remembered something else. "Plus I still need to clean my room. My mom will kill me if I don't. Meanwhile my aunt, who is supposed to be keeping an eye on us, could wake up and decide to drive out here any minute. I doubt she'll show up… she usually leaves us alone, kind of an unspoken thing between us and her, but she could. And that would suck, big time."

Loney was looking at her as if she was crazy. "You may not be able to get to your room."

"I have to! And if we take too long we're going to be driving a corpse around in bright daylight."

"You mean *broad* daylight."

Broad daylight? That didn't even make any sense. "Whatever." Od got an idea. "What about Ed's Body? It's gotta be super cold in the graveyard now. Doesn't it need a sweatshirt or something?" Ed's hemochromatosis would keep him from feeling cold to a point, but only to a point—it wouldn't stop him from literally freezing or getting frostbite. She assumed the same would apply to Ed's Body.

"Actually, yeah, prolly," said Loney.

"OK, so let's go give him a sweatshirt at least."

Od made them all soup. Loney and her ate in her room, away from the slumped Emily Cline and the smell she had brought with her. She put the rest of the soup in a *Jem and the Holograms* thermos for Ed's Body, since it was the only one she could find, and grabbed Ed's green sweatshirt off his bedroom floor. She then put both in Ed's backpack with a can of Shasta Cola.

"Oh crap. I can't leave Walt Disney and Steve Martin in the den—they'll break the accordion door and tear up the couch if they're in there too long." They would.

"So let's put them outside."

"They can't be outside at night. They'll kill Bob's chickens. And he said if he ever sees them do it, he's going to shoot them."

"Can you put them in your room?"

She could possibly, as it was pretty messy in there already. "They're not allowed in the bedrooms by themselves. They destroy everything. The den is the only place they're allowed by themselves, but with Emily in the comfy chair I think they'll break down the accordion door to get her."

"So, what are we doing?"

"You go to the graveyard and give Ed the soup and I'll stay here and make sure Walt Disney and Steve Martin don't get out..." She paused a second. "Or you can stay and I'll go." But Od knew he wouldn't stay—he looked like he was scared of Steve Martin.

15

LONEY

LONEY RODE HIS DAD'S ten-speed back to the graveyard alone and in the dark. He'd realized that there weren't many streetlights out there from their earlier trip to the cemetery, so he found a flashlight in Od's kitchen junk drawer and taped it to the handlebars. He wished he could have taken that stupid baby seat off the back of the bike. It was embarrassing to ride around with it, even if nobody else was awake right now to see it. Plus it was more difficult to balance the bike with it on, and it reminded him of his dad.

ED'S BODY wasn't where they had left it. Or anywhere that Loney could see, for that matter. "Ed!" Loney whisper-yelled into the graveyard, as he ran around the section of the cemetery with the flat grave markers. He ran between the trees and private mausoleums, looking behind each of them. Then he got on his bike and rode toward the front of the cemetery, coasting slowly past the weathered graves, checking in between the shields and crosses and crumbling gravestones, but he didn't see Ed's Body anywhere. He was just about to go back to the newer part of the cemetery and check the community mausoleum when he saw a light coming from across Crest Lane.

Lane Market was a small convenience store that carried an array of different items that someone might not want to go all the way into town for. It closed early and opened late, which Loney always thought was weird, since early morning and late night was usually when people didn't want to make the trip into town, but it had been operational ever since Loney could remember, so they must have been doing something right. They should have been closed now, but the inside was lit up as if it were open.

Loney began to pedal across the street, but just as his front tire touched the asphalt it hit something and the frontend of the bike jerked violently to the left, nearly ripping the handlebars from his fingers. Loney's body seemed to think it should still be going forward so it lurched out of its seat and smashed his sternum into the stem, sending a bright pain through his chest. He groaned, rubbing at the pain. *At least I didn't go over the handlebars.*

When he got his breath back and his feet flat on the ground, he looked down to see what he had hit. It was a good-sized hunk of cement. He stared at it for a moment. It didn't seem to fit or come from anywhere. The street under him, and as far as he could see in both directions, was smooth. Maybe it was part of a tombstone. He picked it up and tossed it under a tree at the edge of the graveyard, then got back on his bike and crossed the road, forgetting the whole thing as the now dull pain faded from his chest.

When he got to the little market, he half expected to find a broken front window and Ed's Body thrashing about inside, possibly smashing things randomly, or flailing wild and belligerent, but the door was simply open, with no visible breakage about. Ed's Body was merely sitting on the floor next to the icebox with six or seven ice cream wrappers laying on the floor next to it. It was currently eating an It's-It, and it had several shades of various treats smeared across its face and clothes. The stench of death oozed from it.

As Loney got closer he noticed it wasn't chocolate or ice cream that was spattered all over Ed's Body, and with each step the smell got worse. *It must have been in the mausoleum.* Loney got a stronger whiff of the stench. *Od's never going to get that smell off that brown chair in her kitchen, or off the back seat of the Buick,* Loney thought. Then he had a worse one.

"Ed's Body...er...Ed?" Ed's Body looked up at him. "Ed, were you in Devotion? The mausoleum." Ed's Body just stared at him. "Ed were you in Emily's *coffin?*" He could just see it: Ed's Body lying down in the empty casket. In Emily Cline's leftovers. Rolling about, rubbing against the rotten satin like a cat. Without a soul Ed's Body must feel like it was a dead body. It had been drawn to where the dead were kept, so it seemed logical that it might try to lie down where they did. "Come on, man." Ed's Body didn't move, except to take another bite of the ice cream cookie sandwich. Loney took it by the arm to tried and lead it away, but Ed's Body started screaming when it was pulled, and swung its free hand at Loney's face. Loney leaned back to avoid being hit, lost his balance and fell on his butt. Then Loney sighed, got up, turned off the lights, and closed the door so nobody would see them if they happened to go by. He sat down on the opposite side of the store so he could barely smell Ed's Body, pushed his shirt over his nose to mask the last bit of smell, pulled his arms inside his shirt, and had himself an Astro Pop.

AFTER ANOTHER IT'S-IT, two Push-Ups, and a sarsaparilla, Ed's Body got up and walked out the door. Loney watched and made sure it didn't get hit by a car on its way across the street, then threw away all of the wrappers and bottles, closed the door, and went back to the graveyard. When Loney made it back he found that the Body hadn't gone back to that grassy area with the flat grave markers like he was hoping. He sighed, cracked his knuckles, and walked as slowly as he could to Devotion. The two front double doors hung wide open.

At first Loney thought that some kind of explosion had gone off in the mausoleum, but there were no burn marks or shrapnel or other such signs of destruction. Then he thought that maybe he was in the wrong mausoleum. Maybe there had been two mausoleums, and he and Od had just missed this one before somehow; this one that was in a state of disarray, construction, or refurbishment. Although that explanation didn't quite fit with what he saw inside either. Loney stepped back outside and looked up. The word Devotion still hung in copperplate letters above the front doors. Loney walked back in and tried to make sense of what he was seeing.

Emily Cline's casket was where they had left it, still open and empty, but there were five...no seven?... no, he counted *nine* more coffins and two urns littering the floor. Five were open, two completely upside down, and two more had been smashed. On the wall pieces of jagged marble still clung to the mouths of the crypts like teeth. A bloated pale-ish man with black spots covering most of his face, and a navy blue suit covering most of his body, lay on his side. Another corpse, the gender unrecognizable, was half in and out of its coffin. One of its arms was completely stripped of flesh, leaving only long wet bones for a limb. It looked as if someone had tried to pull it out, but when the skin and meat began sloughing off they dropped it where it was and let it be. One of the upside down caskets had its lid hinged back as far as it could go, a big splash of black sludge pooling underneath it, as if the body inside had liquified. Loney wondered if the people who ran the cemetery would mop that person up and pour them back into their coffin when they found them, or if they would just throw them away. *Or will I have to make that decision?*

The smell was worse.

As Loney looked up from emptying his stomach of the Astro Pop from earlier he saw Ed's Body sitting cross-legged on the ground, holding hands with somebody in a shiny light brown casket. The hand was withered rather than rotted, but still had some off-color spots. Loney felt a little guilty for giving thanks that they had found Emily Cline in her current condition, but it was a sincere thought, and there was no way they could have gotten any of these others to Odlyn's house in one piece.

Loney was vomiting for a second time, this time mostly Campbell's Chicken Alphabet soup, when he remembered the Vicks VapoRub Od had given him at the house. She had read somewhere that it helped with the smell of the dead. Where she read that or why she had been reading whatever contained that knowledge, he didn't want to know and didn't ask. He unscrewed the top of the container and slathered the rub inside and under his nostrils. He inhaled. It did take the edge off at least.

Ed's Body looked up at Loney, still hand in hand with whomever was in the shiny light brown casket. *What was Ed's Body doing?* It must have been watching them take Emily's coffin out. Maybe it was looking for others like it or looking to belong somewhere. Or maybe it was trying to save or comfort the people like it, or possibly bring them back somehow. Maybe it was just feeling alone. Dang, how did it get the caskets opened and out of the wall… did Od leave the grave-key? Why would she have done that? *Because she didn't think that Ed's Body would start digging everybody up.* She had probably just put it back in the lockbox.

Loney felt a *shift* inside himself. It was unlike anything he had ever felt before. A pull. Or a push. Maybe he was going to throw up again. He braced himself...but nothing came up. The taste of vomit was still stuck to the back of his throat though, so he opened the backpack and cracked the Shasta Cola. He swished it around his mouth and then gargled with it. The soda turned to foam and filled his mouth, making it overflow and spill down his shirt. He pushed his lips together and walked outside to spit it out.

Might as well not add to the mess in there, that he was probably going to have to clean up later. He watched the foam splash against the dirt and took another swig from the can, swallowing it this time.

When he came back inside, Ed's Body was opening another grave in the wall. "Ed!" Ed's Body stopped and looked at Loney for a second and then went back to what it was doing. Loney ran over to him, slipping in a bit of someone, and then tripping over somebody else on the way. He grabbed Ed's Body's hand. "Hey, you can't do that!" Ed's Body blinked. How was he going to get it to—and then the *shift* happened again. Something inside him was stirring. And it wasn't Od's soup or the Astro Pop. Something else. Ed's Body looked at him. *Really* looked at him. As if for the first time. As if it was actually interested. Loney got a strange sensation in his head. A tingling in his fingers and arms. His chest felt bigger. Then he got the urge to bite. He started moving his jaw and baring his teeth and biting the air. He clenched his teeth, grinding them together to try and stop whatever was going on, but it didn't work. He didn't know why he was biting, but he knew one thing. Something was coming out of him.

16

BAD IDEAS

OD DUCK TAPED THE ACCORDION DOOR. It should hold Walt Disney and Steve Martin for a good hour or so at least. She locked the front door too, leaving Emily Cline in the comfy brown chair next to the stove. Her bike was still in the graveyard, so she took the Mongoose, but really, she would have taken the Mongoose even if her bike was here too; it was starting to fit.

Wisner was dark and still, lit only by stars. Most of its houses were built so far back from the road that their lights never made it to the pavement. There was one house at the end of the first turn with a window that looked close enough to cast its yellow light onto the street, but for some reason it didn't. It was as if the light died somewhere between the glass and the road. There must have been a logical reason for it, but this was also one of the spots that Od would always hurry past, even before she had been there at night and saw the dead window light.

After everything Loney had said about his family, and after he confirmed the cat story—which his details had made worse, somehow—the ride down the Scrobe driveway was scarier. It was too dark to see the holes, and the brownish-red spots surrounding them, but she knew they were there, and now she couldn't pretend they were from something else. Her new knowledge also meant that other terrible truths were probably hiding in the dark here.

She stopped the bike and got off carefully, leaning it against the black thing that might have been a tree once again, and walking slowly up that single step—those three important inches that separated her and the rest of the world from where Scrobes lived. Loney made it clear that he wasn't going to let her talk to his mom. He probably had good reasons too. Od's were better though. It did seem like Loney knew what he was talking about—he knew about the scarebox and some other random, weird details—but none of his ideas had actually worked so far. Maybe they would eventually, but she needed Ed back in his body before their parents were home. *Fuck, I just need him back.* She also still needed to clean up the mausoleum and put the Grand National back. Meanwhile there was a dead girl hanging out in her kitchen, who still needed to be possessed, then un-possessed, and then put back into a wall. So Odlyn ignored the horrid feeling that filled her core and knocked on the ill-looking door. The sharp knocks, sharper than she meant, caused something inside to stir. She found herself hoping nobody would answer—just as hard as she hoped that somebody *would*. Her fear screamed at her to flee and she knocked harder, beating the fear into the front door with her fist.

A little boy answered the door.

"Hi…Gatch." Why did it have to be *him*? What was he even doing up? Why did he have one *different* eye? "Can I talk to your mom?" The little boy smiled at her. It made her want to run. It also made her want to smash his face. A strange torrent of emotions fought against each other inside her. She felt so stupid being afraid of a little kid. And embarrassed for it. She felt shame for wanting to hurt him. For wanting to bury him to his neck and…

"You smell like the graveyard."

How could he know that? Even if the stink of Emily Cline's body still stuck to her, how would this little kid know what that smelled like. *This little kid decapitated a litter of kittens.*

"Like a dead girl." Gatch's voice was like a tiny frog that had learned to talk.

She smiled, somehow. "You're so weird. Can I see your mom?"

Gatch led her through the dark living room. The TV was playing a strange black and white cartoon with abnormally long characters drinking out of bottles with X's on them and doing something with knives. It was the kind of obscure, unsettling cartoons they had on in the background of movies sometimes. She could hear the hum of the old television, the crackling of the film transfer, and the brittleness of the foley behind it. Down the walkway to the right that led to the kitchen there was another sound. It was a scraping of some sort, very faint, but definitely there. She didn't look toward it, she just kept walking, the vague smell of mold and neglected carpet hanging limp in the air around her as she went.

Gatch led her down the colorless hallway with the gross white lights that buzzed above. They passed three doors, all closed save one that shut quickly as they passed. The hallway hooked to the right after that door, which she assumed was its end, but then it hooked back to the left after a few more feet and there was another long stretch of empty hall void of doors or any adornment. Now she could see the true end of the hallway and where they were headed. It was a wide door, wider than any Od had ever seen in a house, and it was unfinished and beaten, made of a flimsy brown composite or particle board. It looked as if they had ripped the original frame away and cut pieces of the wall out to fit this new inferior door. It didn't match the hallway. It wouldn't have matched anything. Gatch knocked and swung it open.

There weren't any lights on in the room that Od could see, but as she stepped from the ashen hall and into the swampy dark, she could see the room was bathed in the blue glow of three separate television sets. A long line of dressers wrapped around the room, starting next to the door and continuing to the far left corner. Whoever had placed them paid no mind to the windows or anything else on the walls that somebody might have needed access to in the future. She followed the dressers with her eyes, up and down two and a half walls, and around two corners, to what had to be the largest bed she had ever seen. Lying on the bed was Loney's mother.

If forced to make a guess, Od would say that the woman weighed about five hundred pounds. She was propped up against the headboard in a blue housedress, her hair thrown neatly on top of her head with some type of needle or chopstick. Whether it was the reflection of the televisions, a trick in the lighting, or just plain truth, the woman had the prettiest green eyes Od had ever seen. They contrasted the stench in the room perfectly.

For the first time, Od was grateful to have already witnessed the smell of death. If she had not just spent the earlier part of the night ruining her sense of smell, she might have thrown up right when that crude mammoth of a door first swung open. On the far side of the bed was a pile. She was trying not to look at it. At its rotted food. Its dirty undergarments. Its hunks of this. Its chunks of that. But she could not stop from smelling it.

"Hello, sweetie," Loney's mom said. "Who are you?" Her voice matched her eyes—silk spun from butter. "I'm sorry I can't get up to say hello." Gatch was gone.

"I'm Odlyn. I'm in class with Loney."

"Come sit next to the bed." Her smile was warm.

Od did as she was told. She sat on the hardwood chair across the bed from the pile. *There's no way she could smell the graveyard on Loney. Through this?* Od looked into her eyes. "Your eyes are beautiful," Od said. They were. More so now that she could see them up close. They cut through the blue glow of the TVs and sparkled like the Emerald City.

"Yours are prettier. Silver. With flecks of ruby." Loney's mom leaned in a bit closer. "I misspoke. They are breathtaking."

"Right." Od rolled them.

"You don't see it? You are a beauty." One of her meaty hands reached up and found a lock of Od's hair. "You were made so well."

"Thanks." She believed that Loney's mom believed it. The beauty remark, that was. Whether Od believed it, or whether it was true, was another story. Adults believed some strange and stupid things sometimes. It was as if getting older completely ruined your point of view. "What's your first name?" Od learned a while back that adults weren't used to being asked for their first names by kids. It threw them off a little. Adults were usually always ready. They made sure of it and prided themselves on it, in fact they made sure to make anyone other than themselves feel bad if weren't ready. When you called them by their first names, it took that readiness away for a few seconds. Sometimes it gave a tiny window into who they were.

"Jenny." Jenny smiled. It didn't seem to throw her at all.

"OK. Jenny." No window. Od was just going to have to go for it. "I need to know how to get a soul back into a body."

Jenny chuckled a little. A musical, humming chuckle. "Into their own body?"

"Well yeah, but first I need to know how to get them into a dead body that has been dead for a while that isn't theirs."

"Who?"

"Oh, not Loney, if that's what you're thinking. My brother. I scared his soul out of him. And his body, which can walk around and stuff, went to the cemetery—and now I can't get it to come home and I, uh... well, I got another body and I need to put his soul in that body—"

"So you can bring his soul to his own body."

"Yeah."

"That was Loney's idea?"

"Yeah."

"And he's in the graveyard now?"

Oh shit. "No. He's at my house watching my dogs to keep them away from the body."

"You guys got the body from the graveyard?"

Damn, she was going to get Loney in trouble. "I did."

"Just you?" She raised her eyebrows.

"Well, Ed's Body and I did it... Ed's my brother." Violating her no-lying rule made her stomach feel empty.

"You got the body to dig up another body with you?"

"I got it to help with the heavy stuff. We got it from the mausoleum. I coaxed it with ice cream." Od was so bad at lying.

The pretty eyes of Jenny Scrobe looked into Od's for what seemed to be a long time. "You should have tried to get him to follow you back to your house with the ice cream."

"I tried everything to get him to follow me. He wouldn't leave."

"Listen. Loniel can't go into the graveyard. This is very important."

"Loniel?"

"Loney."

"He didn't."

"I'm very serious, Odlyn. I will help you, but Loney cannot go into the graveyard."

"OK."

Jenny locked her eyes on Od's. More intense than before. Gauging her, Od thought. Od just held the look on her face. She didn't move the slightest muscle, she just kept looking back at her.

"Alright," said Mrs. Scrobe. Od forced herself to tamp down the sigh her body wanted to make. "What you need to do is to go where Ed's soul is and show him where the body is exactly."

"But I was just at my house. I brought the body there and waited. He didn't show up or anything."

"No. You need to go to where he *really* is. He is most likely stuck in a pocket in the house. You have to go into that pocket." Jenny Scrobe started typing on a keyboard that Od hadn't even noticed laying on the woman's stomach. Jenny squinted at a computer monitor that sat next to Od on another hardwood chair. "Do you usually remember your dreams?"

"Yes."

"Good." Jenny put on some archaic glasses and typed a bit more. "Everyone has hundreds of dreams each night. Most people remember a couple at most." She pushed the glasses further up her nose making her eyes grow in size. "Now if I can get you into a dream, and you know you're in a dream," she sounded like Loney as he figured things out on the spot, only she was smoother with it, "I might be able to put you into the pocket Ed is in, in the house."

"OK." Od didn't really understand how that could work. "How?"

"Dreams take place inside pockets, as I call them. These pockets are weaved together in a way that blanket over our waking reality and the afterworlds. We shift between these pockets when we dream. There are also pockets in the afterworlds that lie underneath the dream pockets. They are so close to each other that it is possible to shift from dreams to the afterworlds."

"Afterworlds? Like Heaven and Hell?"

"No…well…no…" Mrs. Scrobe looked over her glasses at Od.

"How do you know this?"

"I've been studying for a very long time."

"Where?"

"I learned bits and pieces from all over."

"Do you know if all of this is true though? Like, how do you know it is actually real? Have you seen the pockets and everything? How do you even begin?"

"I've seen some things and I've done some experiments. I always keep my eyes open, and don't always trust them."

"Why are you telling me all this? You're so…*can't-did* about it all…What if I told other people?"

"The word is 'candid'. I told you because you asked. Withholding information does nothing, but if you share information, you never know how that will help you in the future. Everything comes around." Mrs. Scrobe paused. "As to the other question, you tell me: what if you *did* tell anyone? They'll either think I'm lying, or that you are. Nobody trusts what bedridden fat ladies or little girls say. You have a wild imagination, and I've made poor life decisions." Mrs. Scrobe went back to typing at the computer and then added, "But truth hides in odd places." It wasn't as if she said it to Od, but as if it had just leaked out of her.

"Oh man…" It was as if Od had just found a well of undiscovered knowledge in Mrs. Scrobe. A knowledge nobody else she'd meet would ever have. She could have answers to questions Od had marinating in her for years. "I have tons of questions."

"Sweetie. I can answer everything you want to ask, but I'm guessing that you want your brother's soul back in his body before your folks notice."

"Yeah…" It could wait. Mrs. Scrobe wasn't going anywhere. "What do we do?"

"Well, I'm going to hook you up to this Commodore 64 and see how close I can get you to the house's pocket."

"So the house pocket is different than the dream pockets?"

"Yes and no. A pocket specific to a house doesn't move, and

usually lies underneath the dream quilt. It catches things, spirits, souls, creatures, even dreamers can sometimes fall into house pockets. Dreams kind of do the same thing, but primarily catch dreamers, although they aren't as 'sticky' as say house pockets are... I had a friend who would refer to pockets as spiderwebs, if that helps at all."

"OK." So many more questions sprung into Od's mind. *Why didn't Loney want her talking to his mom? Cause of the graveyard thing?* "So you're going to hook me up to a computer."

"Yes," Mrs. Scrobe said and then matter-of-factly, "It *will* hurt."

"More than the Vampire Game?"

"Yes." Jenny stopped sorting the wires that sprung from the back of the monitor. "They made you play the Game, huh?"

Od held up her finger with the little scabs on it.

"Yes, this will hurt much more. But it's similar. And this time it will be your neck. Not your finger." Od stared. Was this woman going to bite her neck? Would Od let her do that? "Go to the long dresser." Od went. "Open the top right drawer." Od opened it. Inside were dozens of medication bottles, along with a few boxes, and other random things. "Get the long green box and the orange bottle..." They were *all* orange bottles and they all had their labels peeled off. "...with the small, white, *round* pills." Od grabbed the box and the bottle and gave it to Mrs. Scrobe. "Under the bed next to the chair there should be a cardboard box." Od looked and found it—a small moving box without a lid, filled with junk.

Mrs. Scrobe opened the bottle and held it up, twisting it and examining its contents in the light from the TVs. "Alright, take twelve of these."

Alarms started going off in Od's head. "*Twelve*?"

"Yes."

"What are they?"

"They are very mild, natural, sleeping pills. If you take NyQuil or something with chemicals, it'll make your dreams all crazy. You won't be able to concentrate, and I won't be able to get you to the right pocket. In fact, you'll probably just be stuck in your own head until you wake up."

"*Twelve?*"

"Yes. We need you to fall asleep right away and stay asleep. Loney usually takes five at a time on a consistent basis." Nobody knew where Od was. She was warned against coming here from the woman's own son. If she voluntarily took twelve random pills and knocked herself unconscious, this woman could do anything to her. And who knew if they were *actually* sleeping pills? They were in an unmarked medication bottle. Hell, how did Mrs. Scrobe even know what they were? The woman could barely see. There were easily twenty bottles in that drawer. And how common were little white round pills? OK, what was the worst thing that could happen? Well, the woman could be making up all that garbage about pockets, dreams, and afterworlds so that she could knock her out and let her sons rape Od. They'd chop her legs and arms off so she couldn't go anywhere, and keep her in the basement strapped to a table and kept alive with tubes and things so she could bear the new round of Scrobe children. And she would have her own pile to keep her company.

Somebody once told Od that that was a good way of gauging situations: figure out the worst thing that could happen. Maybe knowing that it couldn't get any worse was supposed to be a sort of comfort. The only problem was that Od could think up dozens of horrible things worse than that initial worst. When her mom went to Redville with her aunt to go shopping at a mall and they were a few hours late she would often visualize the car running under a Mack truck and their heads getting chopped off. Their bodies left mangled in the car and their heads still alive for moments, looking around in the dark, wondering what was going on, until the reality dawned on them—that they were only heads now and would be nothing in a few seconds.

When her brother went in to get his teeth checked by the dentist she would imagine him getting pumped with laughing gas and the doctor ripping out his teeth one at a time to see how long Ed would keep laughing. She would see Ed cackling and choking on the blood pouring from his tooth holes, and the doctor letting out a little chuckle of his own as he started in with the saw.

She wasn't a pessimist. She didn't want to think of these things. She tried to fight them from manifesting in her head, but they kept spinning in there, growing into terrifying tragedies she knew had to be true. Until, of course, she found out that they weren't. That didn't matter when her mom was late again, or her dad didn't answer the phone, or her brother spent the night at a friend's house. The tragedies would spin again. She didn't do it on purpose though. Her brain did it.

Mrs. Scrobe was looking at her expectantly. There was one person that Ed had right now. One person that could really help him. Her. Odlyn. "Do you have a basement?" Od asked.

Mrs. Scrobe frowned. "No..."

Od shook twelve pills out of that mysterious orange bottle and swallowed them. It took a few tries, but she did it. Mrs. Scrobe smiled and said, "The antidote to what you just took is hidden somewhere in this house. Now give me the diamond."

"What?!"

Mrs. Scrobe laughed. "It was a joke."

"It wasn't funny." It really wasn't.

Mrs. Scrobe didn't bother apologizing; she just moved on. "The next thing is a bit harder."

"Of course it is."

"You should be asleep within thirty minutes." Mrs. Scrobe

opened the long green box. Inside were all sorts of needles. Long needles. Short needles. Thick needles. Pin-thin needles. All shades of silvers and coppers and bright golds. Loney's mom was wrapping a length of wire she pulled from the moving box around some of them. Then she pulled a metal cube out from that cardboard junk box and fastened the wires to it. "Here." Mrs. Scrobe handed Od some alcohol pads. "Rub this on your neck, away from the jugular."

"Why?"

"Well, I don't have a great deal of mobility. Leaning over that way can be difficult. I was hoping you would do it."

"I'm not stabbing my neck with those needles!"

"You don't have to," Loney's mom pulled a gun from the moving box. A dull metal gun with a groove on the top and a trigger than ran the length of the handle. It looked as if it had been made from spare parts. "You use this." She loaded the top of the gun with a rather nasty-looking needle. A red wire and blue wire were affixed to it somehow and they hung out of the back of the gun.

Od stared at the bad decision presented before her. "Can't I just go to sleep and find him?"

"I need to guide you to where he is. You could be wandering around the tapestry forever and not find it."

"How do *you* know where it is?"

Jenny started to say something and then stopped. "Hmm. Good point. Where do you live?"

"2304 Grey River Road."

Mrs. Scrobe stopped. She pulled her glasses down to look over the rims at Od. "I can see it in you now. N has a very interesting personality...it rubs off on its inhabitants."

"N?"

"Yeah, that's its name. N."

"The house's name?"

"Yes."

"Like the letter?" Just like the comic book.

"Yes. Now I know exactly where to go. I know N."

"Why is it called N?"

Mrs. Scrobe smiled. "Let's get going." She handed Od the Needle Gun.

"How does this work, exactly?" The gun was heavy. It felt dangerous and significant. "Does it *have* to be the neck?"

"The gun shoots the needle into your skin. There is a little flat washer that stops it from going in so far and another thing that keeps it in." Mrs. Scrobe pointed everything out with a pencil as she explained it. "It needs to be long to conduct. The needle is attached to the wire. The wire is attached to the soul box. The soul box is attached to the Commodore 64 so that I can interact with you and get a readout..." Mrs. Scrobe was typing again and frowning. "Hmmm..." Then she looked up. "Oh! Grab the other computer from under the bed. I have a map of N." She smiled and giggled, suddenly pleased with herself. "This is going to be even easier than I thought." She sounded almost giddy.

"Soul box?"

"My own design and construction." Mrs. Scrobe held up the metal cube she had just fastened the wires to. "It allows me to manipulate a soul, talk to it, et cetera." Od could see Mrs. Scrobe's reaction to her own. "It basically lets me interact with you in your dreams."

They set up the second computer right next to the first. The monitor made a click when it was turned on and then a high-pitched whirr that soon faded and merged with the other. There was another box with a semi-transparent lid that Loney's mom made Od retrieve that was labeled, 'Houses'. It was full of alphabetized floppy disks, and Mrs. Scrobe flipped quickly through it and found one with a red 'N' on it. She popped it into the disk drive. Small blocky letters and numbers scrawled across the screen as Mrs. Scrobe typed. Od tried to make out what she was writing, but only caught the end... LOAD "*",8,1... After several seconds a big 8-bit N lowered onto the screen. A few low computerized notes played, then a pixelated version of Od's house faded into existence. Mrs. Scrobe typed something in, hit enter, and the screen switched to a rough map of Od's house. She then turned to the other computer. She typed in something else, and a blank, black screen appeared with a blinking green square. "Alrighty, we're ready to go."

"Where's the jugular?" Od asked, and Mrs. Scrobe told her. Od didn't hesitate. Hesitation was doubt. Doubt couldn't be afforded. Doubt stalled and derailed success. She lifted the gun up to her neck, where Jenny had directed her, and pulled the trigger.

Everything in the room flashed and then blurred, separated, and went back together. It was probably the third-worst pain she had ever felt. She screamed, of course, and a few tears leaked from her eyes against her will. She nearly dropped the gun too, which might have ripped the needle out, but when the gun fell at her side, still in her hand, it tugged at her neck and she held on to it. Loney's mom started typing again and Od felt a shock of electricity explode from the needle. The currents spread like fire across her neck. Streams of electricity multiplied and went through her chest and into her heart, which beat back furiously. Another shock came from the needle and spiraled into her neck. Its live fingers climbed up the back of her head and escaped into her skull. Od's eyes filled up and she could feel herself wanting to cry.

"One down. Two to go." Mrs. Scrobe smiled.

SHE WASN'T JOKING. Od had to shoot herself twice more in the neck. The pain was worse the last time, but right after the last shocks found their way into her body the twelve mysterious pills kicked in. And then she drifted into the... *black landscapes... green...blinking...square...*

IN

"WAH WA WAH WAH WAH." Od wished that is what she heard when Mrs. Rose was up there vomiting her latest lesson. But no, she heard it all. She had a real problem with that. Some kids could go to sleep in class or look out the window and tune out. Not Od. She had a real listening problem. It wasn't so bad in all of her other classes. All the way up to fifth grade with Ms. Parks, Od had found listening bearable, but now that she had Mrs. Rose it was different. Mrs. Rose hated Od. She even dragged her into the hall one day to tell her so. She would even get mad at Od for listening. Wah wa wah wah. "Yes ma'am," Od would say. The Peanuts had it easy.

Od finished drawing the last bit of a unicorn. She drew it to look like it was bursting out of the ruled paper, unconfined to the limits of the blue lines or the flatness of the page, which was trickier than it seemed at first. Drawing tuned her in. If she was drawing she was listening; it let her focus on what was being said and cemented the ideas in her head. Od thought about not drawing in Mrs. Rose's class, so she wouldn't have to listen to that monotonous croak, but then she'd be left staring at those infinitely wrinkled lips and perfectly crappy hair. Her voice wouldn't be a tool for conveying a message, but a muddle of words no better understood than the sound of sneakers trying to escape from five inches of mud. At least with drawing she would be able answer questions, and it wouldn't give Mrs. Rose the satisfaction of embarrassing her in front of the class, even if she had to pay attention to the drivel that dripped from her yellowed chimp teeth. Od could push past it all into the void place, where there was nothing and just drift in the calm, but then she would be called on for sure.

Today they were having class in the gym and the cheerleaders were practicing off to the side. The blackboard was under the scoreboard. Od's friend Katie kept going back and forth, first sitting next to Od and then going to cheer with the other girls. She kept asking if Od would go cheer with them, but Od had to draw so she could listen. All of the cheerleaders were wearing black because there had been a funeral earlier that they were cheering in. Their normal red and white uniforms obviously wouldn't have been appropriate. Od thought of dead cheerleaders for some reason. There was something poetic there she couldn't quite put a finger to. Katie sat down next to her again.

"Od, come on and cheer with us."

"Mrs. Rose is watching me."

"I know, but if you can change into your cheer uniform, you can sneak away and she won't even know."

Katie ran back to the other cheerleaders who were working on something choreographed to Taco's version of "Puttin' On The Ritz". Od looked up at Mrs. Rose who was drawing a coffin on the board. The chalk she used looked like an extension of the teacher's gnarly blanched fingers. Od pulled her backpack from off the back of her chair and pulled her black cheerleading uniform onto her lap. She started pulling her arms into her shirt then tried to put the cheerleading top on without exposing her chest. Everyone seemed to be watching intently as Mrs. Rose began drawing a gravestone.

Her chest was itching like crazy under her bra. Katie said it was 'cause her boobs were growing. Od hoped so. Better that than wearing that stupid thing for no reason, like she felt like she was doing already. She got the top on and looked around her. Loney was in the back drinking soup out of a girl's thermos. At least he wasn't sleeping on his desk as usual. She looked around again and pulled the cheerleading skirt on over her pants. Then she pulled her pants down until they got caught on her shoes. She took the right one off without undoing the laces, then the left. For some reason the left one smelled horrible. Mrs. Rose stopped drawing on the blackboard. A couple of kids started looking around. As fast as she could, Od pulled her pants all the way off and shoved them into her bag. She was pulling her shoes back on when Justin Pepper looked at her in disgust.

"Ughhh," Justin whispered. "Od smells like feet."

"Those *are* my feet."

"Your feet smell like a butthole, then," Justin whispered back.

Everyone was starting to look at her. Plugging their noses. Making disgusted faces.

"Ewww," Maris Domico whispered at Od.

"Ahh, grody."

"Nasty," Christine Powers whispered.

Od finally got her shoes on, smashing the tongue down in one and folding the heel down in the other. Ugh. She tried to wiggle the shoes to fit, to fix the heel and the tongue, but it didn't really work. She looked up at Katie who was in line with the other cheerleaders. Mrs. Rose was now drawing a ghost on the blackboard with long vampire teeth. In the top left corner of the chalkboard was a flashing green square. Od saw her chance and ran to get in line with Katie. She saw two hands go up from a couple of girls as she went. Probably to tell on her. *Bitches.*

"Jeez, this line is crazy." The sign to their right was made to look like a coat of arms. At the center of it there was a red box that read:

Wait Time: 45 minutes.

"Yeah, like 45 minutes."

"What do you want to go on next?"

Od looked across from the line. There was a small manmade lake. Submarines. The monorail. Behind that was Space Mountain. "Let's do Space Mountain after this," Od said to Katie.

Katie smiled. "Yes!"

The line ended up being a lot shorter than it said, and soon they were climbing into the railed bobsleds and shooting into the Matterhorn. The bobsleds rose and fell and whipped around the mountain. Its faux icy tunnels were peppered with patches of crystals growing in primary colors. They lit up as the bobsled-train passed them, and fell dark in their wake.

"Is there a bathroom at the top?" Katie asked as the rollercoaster clicked upwards.

At the top of the mountain yellow eyes pulsed from the dark. Rays of light shot in in streams from fabricated cracks in the walls, and then they found themselves careening into a cavern populated by animatronic Yetis. The bobsled swerved and feigned crashing into an ice wall where the sled hissed to a stop.

They were let out of the bobsled by a teenage ride operator and pointed to a series of steps. Just beside the steps, hidden behind a modest waterfall, were the bathrooms. Od waited as Katie used the bathroom, staring at the basketball floating in the pool the water emptied into. A tiny green square flashed on it.

"Od, you've gotta check this out!" Katie exclaimed and Od followed her into the bathroom. There were three animatronic creatures being stored in there. They towered over the two girls. One was Harold, the Abominable Snowman from the ride, but there was also a Wampa, with one of his arms lying on the floor, wires splaying from his stump, and a Bumble from the *Rudolph the Red-Nosed Reindeer* claymation special. Katie got really excited, jumped up and started swinging off Harold's arm. It promptly cracked and started making a low grinding noise.

"Katie! You're going to break it." On the back of Katie's black cheerleading top was that blinking square. The one from the blackboard and the basketball. As Katie swung, the square started to print green words on her back.

Odlyn. Pay attention.

She did.

Go down the—

Katie jumped off the Abominable Snowman's arm, laughing. "See, it didn't break." Od grabbed her and spun her around to read what was being written on her back. Katie pulled away. "What up, spaz?"

"Turn around."

Katie smiled, did a full pirouette and came back to face Od smiling. Katie was a lot of fun. Unless you were actually supposed to be doing something. "No, really. Turn around."

Katie started laughing. "Again?" She did a double pirouette. Od tried to grab her as she did.

"What are you doing?"

"There's a spider on your back." Od thought she was being smart, but Katie just started screaming and running. "Let me get it! Let me get it, Katie! He's going to crawl into your hair! Stop! Katie, stop! Come here!" Od eventually tackled her to the ground. And pinned her. "Hold still." Katie lay face down on the floor between the mechanical monsters, crying into the polished cement with Od straddling her. Katie's hair had come undone from its cheering ponytail and Od brushed it away to read the words that had appeared underneath.

Go down the hall behind the monsters.
Climb the ladder. Up. Go alone.
Remember, you need to get to N's pocket.

Oh crap. Her memory came flooding into the dream. Ed. Ed's Body. Loney. Emily. Jenny. N. Twelve pills. Needle Gun. She was hooked up to a computer. Was this *really* Katie? Or was her mind making her up? She could feel the knowledge of knowing she was asleep tugging at her, trying to wake her up. Od fought it and slapped Katie's back.

"Got it," Od said. "Stupid spider."

Katie turned. "Where is it? I wanna see it."

"Sorry. Ate it already." Od smacked her lips. Katie laughed. "Hey, wait here. I'll be right back."

Katie made that forced sad face she would make when you did something that she didn't like. It always worked on Katie's dad to make him reverse his decisions, and some other adults and boys, but it almost never worked on Od. Even if she could feel it trying to work inside her. "OK," Katie said. Od got up and ran behind the monsters. It helped to think that that might not actually *be* Katie.

In the corner there was a ladder. She climbed it up into a smaller room inside the mountain's peak—a raw, un-magical skeleton façade made of wooden beams. There wasn't anything in the room except for a wastebasket with a tiny basketball hoop above it and another ladder. She climbed again, into a smaller darker space. Cloth hung everywhere in bunches and strands, brushing against her face and neck. She pulled the fabric to one side and slats of light fell in across her face. She pushed towards the light and the closet doors swung open to reveal her parents' room.

A king-sized waterbed dominated the room as always. Od ran around the bed and went for the door, but when she opened it, it opened to a wall. She threw herself against it and it fell away in gray clumps, revealing the hallway. The hall had always frightened Od. It was a bit too narrow. A bit too long. And it had tall mirrors that hung all the way down its length to the other end where the kitchen was. If you were in Ed's room and looking into the mirror across from it, the mirrors were hung in just a way that you could actually see all the way to the other end of the hall. If somebody started walking from where Od was now, in her parents' room, and you were looking into that mirror across from Ed's room, it gave the illusion that they were walking by the mirror over and over again until they got there. Now the hallway was misty. A paleness had taken over it, and in each of the mirrors was something looking back that was not Od's reflection. She started down the hall.

As she passed the first mirror, the one across from the walk-in hall closet that her mom had filled with shoes and handbags, tiny hands pressed against the glass. She looked into the mirror. The hands were so tiny, but a paleness behind the mirror obscured the rest of whoever they belonged to. As she looked, they reached. And she reached out too. As her fingers touched the glass the tiny fingers pushed out of the mirror and grabbed onto her fingers. She pulled away. But the little creature held on and emerged from the mirror. It was skinny, with fair skin. Humanoid, but maybe only about twenty-five inches tall. Its face was sort of babyish, although the eyes were too small and had no color; just shiny white orbs stuck in gray clay. It choked out a teeny voice underneath a series of wet gurgles and started grabbing at Od.

"No," she said. It mumbled something else and grabbed her legs with both hands. Od backed away, tripped, and fell into another mirror so hard that the thing cracked. The little creature ran off in a blur. More hands sprung from the mirror she fell against, grabbing her face and neck to pull themselves out of the mirror. By the time she pulled herself off the glass and to her feet again, three more of the things used her to climb into the hallway and run into the kitchen. More tiny hands pressed against the opposite side of the mirrors. They palmed the glass and scratched at it with their fingers. It was a terrible sound, like fingernails against slate and teeth on tinfoil. Od ran until she got to Ed's room and then practically dove inside.

Od jumped at seeing the girl sitting on Ed's bed. She was older than her and Ed. Pretty...and pretty much not wearing anything, either. She was as pale as everything else, almost as if she were made of the stuff, and she seemed familiar. Od looked hard at the girl and a word appeared in her head. *Aureolin.* Small tangles of mist floated off the girl and dripped back into the paleness around her. A red light pulsed from her chest and between her legs. It covered her and it filled in the pieces that seeped away when she moved her mouth. Od knew her. Somehow. She didn't recognize her, but she knew her. No doubt of it.

As the girl worked her mouth, nothing came out except for a noise so unlike a voice, almost like something scratching on the wind. As the scratching continued, bits of Aureolin came off of her body and formed a sculpture in the air. It was twisted, slowly spinning, and small. Od looked closer. It was an action figure. Aureolin fed herself into the vision, showing the figure walking through a field of shag carpet, towards Emily Cline. The scratching faded and the pretty girl melted into the Pale.

THE PALE, as she began to call it in her mind, was so thick in the kitchen that it was hard to see. It came up to Od's knees and wrapped tightly around her as she trudged forward. She swished the Pale from side to side with her arms, hoping to glimpse the action figure, but it was no use; just as soon as she shifted the dirty fog more of it took its place, wafting, sliding, oozing in from all sides to keep its position.

Emily Cline was sitting in the comfy chair just as they had left her. She had the same tilt to her head. The same hitch to her limbs. Except now she was…moving. She twitched, or flinched, or moved in some way, it was just difficult to see *how* with the paleness obscuring her. Od waded over to Emily, looking for the action figure as she went. What did Ed have to do with the action figure? They must be connected somehow. Or they were important to each other. The dead girl moved. Again, a twitching kind of movement. Od moved closer, attempting to focus past the Pale. What was she doing—what was making her move? Was it Ed taking possession of her? Was he—and then she realized—*Oh god*. Steve Martin was eating the dead girl.

"No!!" Od yelled. Trying to scold the dog. "Bad dog! Don't eat her!" She tried pushing the Pale to the side. "Steve Martin!" But she couldn't see him anymore. Maybe it was Walt Disney that was trying to eat her; now she wasn't sure. "Walt Disney, no! No!" She couldn't let them eat her…she couldn't leave without Ed though. But even if she did find Ed, Emily was his ride out of here. "ED!"

There was movement all around her in the pale of the air. It was shifting and flowing between her and Emily. Then Od saw the action figure in Emily's shoe. It was moving its arms and legs; then it stopped, and Emily Cline's head moved in a purposeful way. Something clicked in Od's head. She shouldn't be there. She needed to be back in the house. Out of this dream. "Jenny!" But there was no answer. "Mrs. Scrobe!" Maybe she couldn't hear her. Od was probably just a little yellow square on Jenny's map of N on her computer. "Fuck! Come on!"

The blinking green square popped into view. On the stove next to Emily.

Brace yourself...

Od's head and chest exploded as three pulses ripped through her, one right on top of the next. All of the air went out of her and all of the Pale sucked in on itself. Od inhaled deep. The gray folded into black and...she woke up in the chair next to Mrs. Scrobe's bed.

Od gulped down big mouthfuls of air. She stood up and pulled the needles out of her neck. Then she noticed more wires sprouting from her chest. She ripped those out too. Mrs. Scrobe must have put them in while Od was asleep.

"Did you get to talk to him?"

Od was still trying to get more air. "I...I...I..." Od tried to form words, but couldn't talk yet. "You..." Od reached up to her chest. "You..." More air. Od stumbled to the door and pulled it open. "My dogs...they're...eating the girl," Od got out finally. She turned, knocked into the dresser by the door and fell. Pain suddenly bloomed in her hip, but she ignored it, getting up, and—she noticed something sticking out from behind the dresser. Something that she assumed had fallen when she hit it. It was one of the comic books. She grabbed it and ran down the hall without looking back.

She was out the front door and grabbed the Mongoose, pedaling as hard as she could down the driveway. She took a right onto Wisner and felt the tires grip the asphalt. She went faster. She could swear she could see the tops of the pines starting to show up against the sky. She pedaled harder. Left on Grey River Road. Left into her driveway. She jumped off the bike and let it keep going as she ran to the front door. Then the door was open and she was through the front room. She turned left again into the kitchen area. There was Emily Cline. She was waving her arms at the dogs who had broken through the taped doors and were running back and forth, barking at her. "Ed?" said Od.

Emily Cline looked back at her. She had popped the stitches that held her eyes closed and behind were dark sunken circles. Emily tried to say something to her...but it came out as, "mmmm mmmuuu...ullllu uuhhhhhh...nnnngggg." Then Emily closed one eyelid. A wink? Od smiled. It was Ed. She flung her arms around Emily Cline's body and squeezed. Something snapped underneath the dead girl's dress. It seemed to release more of that dead-smell. Od inhaled, let go, and gagged at the ground. Up came some of that alphabet soup, including full-on letters that hadn't yet been digested. She saw an "L", an "O", and an "N" next to each other and it made her wonder where Loney was, and if his mission to the graveyard had been successful. Walt Disney braved getting closer to the dead girl to lick up Od's puke. Steve Martin continued to bark, bouncing back and forth on his front paws.

The doorbell rang.

Od tried to push Walt Disney away from the vomit, but not too hard, honestly it was easier than cleaning it up. She wiped her mouth and went toward the front room. *Who the fuck was at the door...?*

18

GO FIGURE

TUNNELS... Ed remembered tunnels. But that was distant... long ago...

It took Ed a long time to learn to talk again, and even then it was more of a rasping shape of words. And the walking and moving took just as long. The trick was not to think of it the same way he did when living. They weren't body functions; they were projections of will. Just as the thinking itself was. It felt like days, or weeks, before he had a good enough handle on the talking and walking to do anything, but Ed had a feeling that in the living world it wasn't as long. In the meantime, the glowing girl stayed with him. Aureolin was her name, or at least that was the feeling of her name. They would move around each other in a sort of dance. Drift through rooms together. Anything to share the same space. They played with the bits and animals stuck in this place too. She also liked to lay inside of him. That felt unlike anything Ed had ever felt—so un-physical.

It was weird how talking with the Are was effortless and how here it wasn't. He thought that maybe they imposed the talking on him. As if they opened a sort of frequency that allowed him to communicate with them. Maybe it wasn't even talking at all, but just felt that way because it was the only frame of reference he had for such a detailed exchange of ideas.

Aureolin pushed a knot of emotions at him. He was beginning

to understand them better and could push his own clumsy ball of emotions back, but he was not anywhere near adept at the new skill. He thought that it might be a more sophisticated form of communication than talking, since it conveyed pure emotion, thought, and intention, and didn't have to be bound by words, but it would take a long time to become competent at it and far longer to master.

The knot she pushed at him now suggested the surroundings, the immediate surroundings, but not the room, a bigger structure. Veins of fondness ran through that and twined around him. Or more specifically, the thought of him. He thought she was telling him that the house liked him.

He pushed surprise, with pockets of amusement back at her.

She smiled.

He smiled back.

Aureolin gasped. The outsides of her quivered. Light drained from her eyes and leaked onto her cheeks and brows, dripping down her face and up into her hair. There was a knot building in her that he could feel before she pushed it. The ambient energy of which was dark and sad.

It hit him.

It was a mess. An ending. A place where you were nourished. Fear. Suddenness. Love. Ending of love. But not hate. Sadness. Pain. Shock.

Ed tried to deconstruct it and put it together in a way that made sense.

She pushed it at him again, but it was more refined. Sanded down.

He fit the pieces together and put words to them. Kitchen. Something of love ended in the kitchen. Sadness in the kitchen. And there was pain. But pain for him. She was having pain *for* him.

She pushed again, filling in the gaps.

Death in the kitchen! No, more singular. Confined.

There was a dead *girl* in the kitchen. Aureolin could feel her.

"Is it Od?!" Those were actual words tearing from his mouth in a ponderous chunk.

Aureolin threw a helplessness. A confusion. She didn't know.

Ed started fizzing and popping.

She pushed her sad away and sent him more. Emptiness. Raw. Fact. Knowledge. Simplicity. He thought she was telling him that he did not have a body anymore; warning him of it.

Mouths with sharp teeth started opening all over his body— no, his soul. They began gnashing their teeth and emitting low, guttural screams. Ed's eyes fell back and a yellow light pulsed from his sockets.

She pushed possibility. Hope. It might not be Od.

"WHO ELSE WOULD IT *BE*?" all of the mouths growled together.

Finality. End. Fire. Worry. Finality again. She was telling him to stop. That he would burn up, or burn out?

But he couldn't stop. He could feel himself gathering energy from the house. Gathering energy from something that moved below him. From Aureolin. He tried to move toward the kitchen, but couldn't. The energy was cumbersome. It was as if the lines of energy were ropes, tied to him, strengthening him, but holding him down. He ripped one foot forward, but that was it. And it wasn't very far. That couldn't be Od. IT COULDN'T!

Stop. Focus.

"I can't," squeaked a little mouth near his ribs.

Empty. Funnel. Conduit. Drain the energy into something else.

"How?"

Focus. Focus. Focus. Self. Core. Focus.

But he couldn't do it...draining...he couldn't see...sooooooo anggggggryyyyyyyy...so scared...just too much of everything...and then there was something else.

What was that? Ed could see a way out. A way for his soul to get out of the pocket. Like a back door, a secret passage. With all the energy wrapping around him, feeding him, feeding *into* him, it made everything brighter. The Pale was dimmer and the waking world was bright. Currents of light, electricity, and frequency were running between certain things. It was the spirit he was drawing from the house and from below his room and from Aureolin that made him able to see and allowed him to feel that once he took that back door, the energy would snap off of him and fold in on itself. But he needed something to highlight. Something to drain into. He wouldn't be draining the energy. That wasn't the way. There was too much of it. He would be draining his soul into something else that the energy couldn't go into. He looked around the room as best he could. Too bad he wasn't in his closet; there were tons of things in there. A mouth opened on his thigh so wide that it tore his leg from him. The mouths moaned in unison.

He was vaguely aware of Aureolin trying to tell him something. Screaming, even. He needed something shaped...so he could move. Like a stuffed dog or an action figure. His soul was tearing apart. Bits peeling away as the mouths of his emotion screamed. Maybe a Hot Wheels car would work. Little ribbons of Ed were peeling off and floating into nothing. Why had he put all of his toys away, dammit?! That would teach him to clean his room. Aureolin was melting...crying...no, not Aureolin, *he* was melting...he was...almost completely gone...but...

He saw something close enough. Behind the dresser. An action figure. He used the back door, the secret passage, a sort of electric tunnel, and slung himself into it. He could sense the energy snapping back to the house as his soul poured into the action figure, inhabiting its chest, head, and limbs, filling the plastic and the poorly articulating arms and legs.

HE DID IT. He had made it into whatever action figure this was. Ed was going to have to learn to move all over again. In this...*who was he*? He managed to look down at the figure he had...*possessed? Was that the right word?* Of course. Of all eighty-four of the action figures it could have been, it had to be this one. He shook his little plastic head. There was a reason this figure got smashed off the top of the dresser by one of the Ninja Turtle's ninjatos and was never recovered or regrouped with the others. He was the first to die in every toy fight. He had been thrown off that dresser by Skunkor, Snake Eyes, She-ra, an angry mob of Ugnaughts, and countless others before that blue bandana-ed Ninja Turtle took him out for the last time. He was the throw-away. The first to die. The expendable. Now instead of getting to run around as a Transformer or Boba Fett, Ed was stuck in a fat bounty hunter named Dengar. *Man, couldn't it have at least been Zuckuss?*

It took some time to learn how to even stand up as an action figure. Especially this top-heavy, tiny-legged one. Dengar didn't have any knee joints or elbow joints, and the joints that connected the legs to the torso only swung back and forth. He fell over nine times until he started using the molding at the bottom of the wall to help. Ed caught sight of his bed at one point and imagined lying in bed, seeing the little Dengar action figure first wiggling his legs and arms in the air for God knows how long, then trying to stand up and falling over and over and over again. He thought it would be hilarious. Well, probably freaky at first, but after he realized the thing was having such a difficult time trying to stand, it would become funny. He wondered if Aureolin could see him. Since he was in the living world now, he couldn't see or feel her.

Now that the energy had snapped back into the house, his emotions had reset. He was almost as he had been when he was first pushed from his body by the scarebox. Kind of apathetic. He knew he had a purpose though; he had to get to the kitchen and find the dead girl. And make certain whether it was Od or not. *But if it wasn't her, who was it, and why was she there?*

IT WASN'T EASY to navigate the shag carpet in his room or the single step down into the hallway, which was also covered in shag. Trying to walk in shag carpet that came up to your waist, with legs that didn't bend at the knees or articulate at the hip, was nearly impossible. Sure, the carpet made it easier to stand his figures up in when he was playing with them, but as an action figure it was ridiculously hard to walk in, like wading through quicksand. Once he got onto the linoleum it was a little easier, but it became a whole different type of balancing act. The floor in the kitchen, although thankfully flat, was much slicker than he remembered it being and he fell more times than he could count. *Stupid Dengar*. This had to be the most top-heavy action figure he had, with the most disproportionate leg to body ratio. If only he had left the G.I. Joes out he was playing with a couple days ago. They had much better joints and articulation. Ed made a silent vow to never again clean his room.

It must have taken him an hour or three to get out to the kitchen and see the dead girl, who was most definitely not Od. Whoever she was, she had been dead for a long time. Why was she here though? There was what looked like a note on her, but Ed couldn't read it. First it was too far away, and then when he got close enough to read, it became obscured by the angle and a ruffle in the girl's dress. He was going to have to climb up to it.

He tried climbing up her shoe, but he couldn't close the hands on the plastic of the action figure, and her shoes were patent leather which made it like climbing ice. On his eighth attempt, he got as far as the strap before falling, and that turned out was his best. He didn't get tired in the plastic body, since there weren't any muscles to get tired, no breath to run out, or blood to pump, but the limitations of the plastic was frustrating and that frustration was as powerful as any fatigued muscles or empty lungs could ever be.

After his thirty-seventh attempt to climb the dead girl's leg, Ed lay on the ground, in the plastic figure, staring out toward the den and meditating on his failure. The linoleum gave way to more shag carpet, its giant blue ropes laying this way and that, timber and askew, giving the illusion of an alien jungle. Beyond that the accordion doors to the den rose massive to the sky-far ceiling, threatening that they could be holding back something grander and much more frightening than Kong. They were shut. That was weird. And duct-taped. That was weirder. He thought of how Od still thought it was called *duck tape* and got the urge to laugh.

The accordion doors began to move at the bottom. It looked like they were being pushed at from the other side. Was somebody locked in there? Od? He got up and started the journey to the doors, climbing into the thick foliage before him. The bottom of the doors pushed out again, and there in the distance, pushing through the bottom of the door was a colossal snout. It pushed harder and forced its way out. White fur followed. It was Steve Martin.

Ed tried to smile, but the plastic didn't allow it. He loved that dog. He would love to put his arms around his furry neck and bury his plastic face in fluff, to cling to his neck or tuck into his collar and ride him through the house. Steve Martin pushed his head through the bottom of the door. For a second he thought somebody must be coming from behind him and he tried to turn, but then he realized that Steve Martin was looking at him. He had never been the recipient of that look. He had seen it many times on the dog's face, but never from this perspective. Steve Martin wanted to eat him. The dog tried to push through, but his collar got caught on something at the bottom, so he pulled his head back behind the doors again. His paws replaced it, digging at the base of the doors. The tape was holding for now, but Ed knew it wouldn't last so he started to run.

It wasn't much of a run. More of a run in intention than in execution. He could hear the dog behind him breaking through. The duct tape was giving way and the accordion doors were coming off their track. Ed managed two more steps and then the doors broke apart and he was in Steve Martin's mouth. The dog shifted Ed to the back right part of his jaw and chewed. The bites didn't hurt, thank God, but he could feel his body being misshaped as the teeth pushed into him. What would happened if the dog chewed him to bits? Or what if he was swallowed?

The dog spit him out to get a better look at what he was gnawing at and pawed him. Ed used the momentum to get up somehow and was 'running' again. He made it behind the girl's leg without getting caught and attempted to climb the back of her left shoe. It was no use, so he pushed off the bottom of the brown spinny chair and threw himself *into* the girl's shoe. *Her shoes were at least a size too big for her, thankfully. Maybe feet shrank when you died.* Steve Martin, now accompanied by Walt Disney, was right behind him, but they would only come so close to her. If it wasn't for their fear of the girl, he would have already been eaten.

What a horrible way to die, Ed thought. Eaten by your own dogs. The ones you trained and named. Not that he named them very well. Od and Ed had first named the dogs after themselves. Od named hers Ed and Ed named his Od. Their parents vetoed that and told them to come up with something different, so they named them Who and What. They used another veto on that one too, saying it would be too confusing, obviously not realizing that that was the joke. "Think of something that fits them," they said. So Ed named his Steve Martin because of his great sense of humor and comedic timing and Od named hers Walt Disney because of her little gray mustache. Ed's parents thought that they were done with the theme of giving their animals proper first and last names after Steven Spielberg, but Ed liked the tradition and if they ever got another cat he wanted to name it Whoopi Goldberg.

Steve Martin was doing his dance, edging closer to the girl's foot and then backing up, testing his fear and whether or not the girl was going to strike, but it didn't take long for him to screw up enough courage to start nosing the chair and then the girl's shoe. When he couldn't nose Ed out of that shoe, he started to bite. Walt Disney, meanwhile was contributing a constant stream of barks from behind.

When Steve Martin finally got up enough nerve to latch onto her foot, the dead girl moved. Ed thought that it was because the dog had jerked her from position, and it might have been, but when he looked up from the shoe, which had now been pulled out from under the dead girl and was in a sort of kicked-out position, he saw past the blue ruffles and could have sworn her head was swiveling in an almost deliberate way. Steve Martin ran from her and Walt Disney continued to hop and bark. Ed jumped ship. He slipped and fell and ran and slipped and fell again and then turned to see the dead girl. Had she moved? She had, hadn't she? Of her own volition? No, it must have just been because she was pulled by the dog. Her arms fell from her laps to her side. Maybe settling? He turned and ran again, spilling to the floor and sliding on the linoleum until he faced her again. She was still. The dogs were still barking at her, daring to get closer a couple steps at a time. Then Ed saw the note. Her position made it easy now.

Ed.

Possess this girl.
We'll explain later.

Only Od could have written that. But why did it say "we"? Who was the *we*? Unless of course she was referring to the dead girl. Ed didn't put it past her. His sister would totally include the dead girl in her "we". When they took walks in town and the worms would be out on the sidewalk after the rain or after the sprinklers, she would pick them up and put them back in the dirt, away from being baked to the cement or squashed by clumsy feet. She had a soft heart for life. *And death, I guess.*

But where was Od? Why the note? Why was this dead girl moving? And a dead *girl*, Od? Seriously? And where was *Od*? Ed shut the questions up. This action figure didn't want him in it. Ever since he went into it, the plastic was trying to push him out. But could he even get into the dead girl? He could kind of remember how he got into the action figure—it was kind of like feeling around in the dark though, and he didn't have the house's energy to channel and propel him anymore. Maybe it wasn't entirely necessary. He looked at the girl, shifting his gaze, and focused past her.

He saw it. It was close. There was an opening. A corridor. A closing door. *Is it a way* into *her?* Ed stopped thinking and dove.

19

BERNIE

BERNIE DIDN'T WANT TO BE THE BAD GUY. He was just "pulsive." He would get something in his head and the next thing he knew he was doing it before he had actually decided to or not. It felt like that was what happened earlier and he had been up all night thinking about it—Ed moving the monkey with his mind, Od saying that they could do more than that, Ed saying that Bernie could probably do it too, and he, himself, moving the drawer with his mind—it all seemed like his "pulsiveness," but harnessed for good…well, for a specific goal, anyway.

Now that he had these powers, he was going to have to stop taking things. He'd have to try to stop breaking stuff too. He had to right his wrongs. He knew that in this world, great power came with big responsibilities. He read that in an old comic book of his uncle's. A comic that Bernie had snuck out of its protective bag and drawn some expertly crafted mustaches and goatees in. And if Bernie was going to be added to the roster of those with great power, if Bernie was going to become a hero in this world, he would start by correcting the crappy things that he had done. No matter how small. That is why Bernie had come back to the Perfect house. To begin righting his wrongs. It made too much sense not to have his first correction be here, where he had gotten his powers. Returning something he had taken to the person he'd received his powers from was like a poem; it was "a poetic", as they said. So he rang the doorbell. Tonight he would give Od back her stolen underwear.

Od and Ed's parents were supposed to be back sometime in the morning, so he knew he wouldn't be waking *them* up, and he did not want to do this with them around. There was a difference between doing the right thing, and doing a stupid thing. No need to bring grown-ups into this.

He had it worked out already. When Od or Ed answered the door, he would ask to talk to Odlyn alone and then give them back to her and just say he was sorry. She would ask why he took them and he would... *Crap.* What would he say? She would be so pissed and weirded out. Maybe he didn't have it totally worked out yet. Oh well, it didn't matter. He was supposed to do what was right, no matter what. He had a great power now. Or was on his way to it. Great power didn't steal underwear...but if great power stole underwear before it had become great power…it would give them back…right? He was getting confused. He wished somebody would open the door already. He was starting to feel really weird waiting at the door holding a pair of his cousin's panties. He rang the doorbell again.

The dogs had been barking ever since he rolled up on his bike. Stupid bike. Not only did it have a big purple banana seat, and not only did he have to get it from the thrift store, but it wouldn't brake correctly either. He tried painting it black with his brother's "special" art set, the one he'd saved for, for three months, but after only one day of rain the paint peeled off. Then after that, the paint flakes, or whatever, got into the gears and caused it to make a horrible noise every time he rode it. It was messed up. Although, he'd have to admit, the banana seat was kind of fun to sit in.

He had never come out here making that stupid bike noise at night before, so the dogs were probably just being protective. He wished he had a dog. His parents wouldn't let him though; they changed their minds after the cat lost its eye. Even though it wasn't his fault. It was an accident.

There was a sound from behind the door. Somebody was coming. He was going to right this. The door unlocked. Now was his chance to take on the first right in his long line of saving people; this is where he was going to become a hero. This was Day One. Minute One. This was history. Ground zero, as they said. The door opened and Bernie shoved the underwear into the kangaroo pouch in his hoodie. "Uh, hi Od."

"Bernie? What the hell?"

"I, uh..." *Excuse. Excuse. Find an excuse.* "I came here... er… good morning!"

"Dude, it's still dark outside."

"Oh man, what's that smell?" It was a vague smell, but sort of heavy and sick.

"Why are you here?"

"I came for...my training." Od looked at him, confused. "You know, like in the kung fu movies and books where somebody gets magic powers and stuff? They always come to start their training so early that the sun isn't up yet... So, I'm ready to learn the ways of the Force. To learn the not-magic." He smiled.

"Bernie, listen...I...come over tomorrow, OK? I'm busy."

"Sleeping?"

"Uh, yeah. I'm busy sleeping and you woke me up. Go home."

"Wait there's something else. I...uh...I..."

"Bernie. Tomorrow."

"No...uh...I have to..." Bernie fumbled in the kangaroo pocket. "I have this great responsibility." He cracked his knuckles and looked down. "...uh."

"Seriously Bernie, this can wait until tomorrow. Trust me." And behind Od, another girl walked out from the kitchen area to the front room. She had a dress on. A bit dirty though. *Oh.* Bernie got it. She was having a slumber party and didn't want him around. He felt kind of stupid…But also like he kind of wanted to come in. How many girls were in there? He smiled. "Hey!" He called out to the girl in the blue dress. When she turned he saw her face. There were black spots on it...and...there was something wrong. Something with her eyes...and her mouth…she looked sick…and she was missing part of her lips! Bernie screamed.

20

LIES

OD SPUN AROUND AND SAW Ed in Emily Cline's body shambling about behind her. "Ed!" He probably didn't have a whole lot of control of this new body. She turned back to Bernie who was wide-eyed and still screaming. "Bernie! Be quiet!" But he was backing away now and screaming louder. She took a quick look around outside and grabbed him, having to throw all of her strength into it to pull him inside.

She managed to slam the door shut and wrestle him down into the sunken living room, pinning him to the ground, with skills she attributed two quarters to having an older sibling, one quarter to living in the Dannoven House, and one quarter to the wrestling with Katie when they were little.

"Bernie." First thing she had to do was get him to shut up. "Bernie, I'm gonna slap you like in the movies." So she did. "Now shut up." It worked. The movies hadn't lied to her there, although she did kind of feel like a cliché. "Bernie. This is Ed."

Bernie's chin was quivering. "He's in a...costume?"

"Yes…" She couldn't do it. Once you lied you had to keep it up, then you had to keep up the keeping up, and then keep track of the whole mess. She saw her aunt do it all the time, like it was fun for her; like it was some sort of demented mind circus and she had all these rings going, and she was all, 'Look at what I can do'. Playing the joke on Bernie about having telekinesis was one thing.

They meant to tell him about that right afterward and they *would* tell him about it when this whole thing was over; it had just been a joke. This lie wouldn't be justified, and even if it was it didn't matter; Od couldn't lie again. She already did it to Mrs. Scrobe about Loney going into the graveyard, and she had weighed that against Ed's life. It was a necessary evil—the phrase felt like an oxymoron in her mind. This? This was Bernie. A kid. Her cousin. She could handle Bernie, and she thought he might react to the truth, as crazy and weird as it was, better than a lie. "No. It's not a costume. That is a dead girl from the cemetery. Ed's soul is in her. It's a really long story, but basically I'm trying to save Ed's life." Kids were lied to enough already.

Bernie sniffed. He looked at the dead girl who was watching them. Then he looked back at Od and said, "Can I help?"

"No."

"I can. My powers will come in handy."

"Bernie, you don't have any powers."

"Hey, I know that they're not very strong yet. I mean, I just got them, and to be honest, I haven't really gotten them to work very well since earlier..."

"Bernie..." But in all honesty, maybe everything would be easier with another person. Even if it was Bernie. He was sincere at least. "Alright. But you can't tell anybody."

"I didn't tell anyone about the powers, did I?"

"I don't know."

"I didn't."

First thing first. She was going to get hell from her mom, but she put the dogs in her room. Then she put the scarebox in her backpack along and the action figure she found lying next to the comfy chair. She decided that Ed must have been in the figure and had to use it to get out of the pocket and into Emily. Things would have been much simpler and easier if she had known he could just go into an action figure and it would have crossed a couple felonies off her Had Done list. She was pretty sure that it was a Star Wars figure, but it wasn't a very cool one. It was a fat guy with bandages around his head. Not that being fat excluded one from being cool. She knew that girl named Charlene who was fat, and she was one of the coolest girls Od ever knew. There must have been a better word than "fat" that was nicer, but she couldn't think of it. Maybe she shouldn't even think about that aspect of people, it was their business, not hers. She was baffled with Ed's choice though; out of all the action figures he had, why he would choose this one? She thought that, had it been her, she might have gone for the Inspector Gadget figure. He was bigger, had a telescoping neck, and a bunch of helpful doodads. Od picked up her backpack and added a few more supplies, a lighter, one of her dad's pocketknives, and another Shasta Cola.

After a couple tries it was obvious that the Ed-Emily creature couldn't ride the Mongoose. Too bad Loney's bike was in the graveyard, 'cause they might have been able to put Ed-Emily in the baby seat. The thought made her chuckle and Bernie gave her a look. Oh well. She had the Grand National, even if she did feel that driving it again was pressing her luck. *No Whammy, No Whammy, Stop!* Bernie called shotgun and sat up front, and the Ed-Emily thing sat in the back with its seat belt on.

21

DEATH ROOM

AS THEY PULLED UP BEHIND the mausoleum Ed-Emily groaned and tried to say something. "Ngguuuhh," he/she said.

"Word," Bernie said in agreement.

"Mmmnngggg," Ed-Emily replied, trying to move.

That's when Od saw him in the headlights. Ed's Body. Holding its head in its hands as if in pain. Od undid her seat belt and hopped out of the car. She was going to call to it, but wasn't sure what to call it. Ed's soul was in the back seat inside Emily, this was Ed's Body. She got closer and it looked up at her. "Od?" It straightened up and let go of its head for a second.

It was talking to her. And it knew her name. How did it know her name? "Ed?" she said.

"What?" It looked confused, staring at Od with the headlights shining behind her. She must have been just a silhouette to it.

"How did...what are...Are you OK?" Od didn't know what to say, or how to say it.

"I'm OK...I just don't know...Oh, I feel nauseous." It grabbed its head again. "Aggh, my head hurts so bad."

Od looked back at the Grand National as Bernie was getting out of the car. Ed-Emily was staring from the back seat. *What was going on?* "What—what happened?"

"I went back into the mausoleum after we went to the store and I started to feel really weird. Ed's Body had pulled all the bodies out and I was yelling at him and then...it felt like something was coming out of me."

"...Loney?"

"Yeah... I just came out of my body. I tried to grab on, and...I held on for a bit, half in and half out of my body. It was so weird— my soul was hanging out of my body, but I could still work my arms and legs... it was the strangest sensation. I could see..." He squinted as he trailed off. "Anyway, I started slipping out and saw my body slumping and tried to jump back in, but I just kind of slingshot myself into Ed's Body somehow. I thought I could just jump back into my body, and tried to, but it collapsed."

Od stared at him. She didn't know what to say. It was like he had witnessed his own death in a way. Was that what it was like for Ed? For everybody?

"Hey," said Bernie. "Uh, so is this not Ed?"

"No," said Od. "Ed is in the car. This is Loney."

"Loony Loney?"

Loney-Ed flipped Bernie off.

"Sorry…" Bernie said. "Where's *your* body?"

Loney-Ed sighed.

Od was thinking things were getting to be like that game where you have to guess which ball was under which cup. The comparison did not give her any comfort. That game was a street magic trick to take people's money. Nobody ever won.

"Hey, uh, Od. I think that the Ed-girl needs help getting out."

But instead of letting Ed-Emily out of the car they all got in so they could sit down and figure out what to do. Bernie and Loney-Ed wouldn't get in the back with Ed-Emily though, so all three of them packed into the front seat.

"Guys…she smells *so* bad," Bernie said.

"We know, Bernie. You've said it a hundred times since we left my house."

Loney-Ed was still rubbing his head. "I've never had my head hurt this bad."

"I think you mean *Ed's* head," Bernie said.

"That's not helpful," Od said and gave Loney-Ed some Tylenol that she always kept in her backpack. She wasn't a stranger to headaches. She also pulled a second container of Vicks out of her bag for all of their noses.

Loney-Ed sighed. "OK, I think I have something that might work. What we need to do is have me and…and...uh…" he looked in the rearview mirror at Ed-Emily, who was still fumbling with the seat belt and pointed at them. "Ed-Emily and I will go into Devotion. I'll open the scarebox. It will scare me out of Ed and Ed out of Emily and then Ed will go back into his body."

Od wasn't convinced yet. "What about you?"

"I think my body is...OK. I should be able to get back in too." He rubbed the top of his head, then his neck. "It had a pulse. I think I just sort of messed up before trying to get into it."

"If you open the box, who's going to close it?" Od asked. "I opened the box last time and nothing happened to me. And how do you know it's going to scare both of you out? Maybe you have to be in front of it for it to work on you."

"When I get back into my body, I'll close it. If I need to I can turn the box around for it to work on me too." Loney-Ed looked like he was going to puke. "Both of us don't belong in these bodies…This one definitely doesn't want me in it, at least."

Bernie got excited. "Maybe I can open the box with my powers from outside. I can close it too."

Loney-Ed looked at Bernie, frowning. "Your powers?"

"Yeah!" Bernie said. "I have powers like Od and Ed...oh, or you can do it, Od."

Od shook her head at Loney-Ed about Bernie. "Bernie, I can't move the box with my powers."

"Then I can do it." He was excited.

Od sighed. She pulled out the scarebox. "Move the box, Bernie."

Bernie squinted at it. Twitched a little. It just sat there. Bernie squinted harder. Raised his hand and twitched harder. "It's not working."

Od sighed. "Loney, I'm opening the box. I opened it before and nothing happened to me. Then you both can be in front of it and then I can close it right away."

"What if your soul gets scared out?" Loney asked. "Then what? Who will save us?" They both looked at Bernie who was still squinting at the box, moving his fingers in little squiggles at it. Loney looked back at her.

"I won't get scared out. I didn't before."

"If it doesn't work *my* way," Loney said, "we can do it again."

"Liar. I read this." Od pulled the comic book she had found in Mrs. Scrobe's room out of her backpack. "It says that the more a soul is scared out of a body the more frightened it will be of bodies. We can't do this over and over again. Your souls might not go back."

"Afraid of bodies? Where did you get that?" Loney-Ed grabbed the comic book. It read:

The Scarebox, Issue #2

"I took it... from…"

"My house? But I've never seen this one. This is issue two." He flipped through it to find the part she was talking about. There on page eleven was a panel near the bottom that read,

"If scared from a body too many times, the soul, although maybe not consciously, may become frightened of bodies and may not

enter any *body. Or simply may not be able to anymore. Too many times may be once, or twice, or possibly even more than three. It depends completely on the particular soul and body and situation."*

Loney-Ed grabbed his head again and moaned. "Where in my house?"

Od couldn't—wouldn't—lie. "Your mom's room... she doesn't know I took it. Well, she might. I saw it when I was leaving and her glasses were off...I thought it would be helpful...there were more there too." She had seen others pinned behind the dresser.

"She gives them to me one at a time as presents. Pretty coincidental that you found that. I..." Loney-Ed stopped. Realized. "What were you doing in my mom's room? Od, she didn't... why were you there?"

"To find out how to get Ed into Emily. She knew. And I did it." It *was* pretty coincidental that she found it then, but throughout her life she had noticed that the closer she got to strange things, like her house, the more coincidences would occur. Of course, it may have not fallen just then, maybe Mrs. Scrobe had Gatch put it there for her to find for some reason. But why?

"No, no, no. You shouldn't have done that." Loney was shaking his head in his hands.

"It's OK. I told her you didn't go into the graveyard."

"No. What did you...? How did you get him in Emily?"

"She hooked me up to the computers. And put me in N's pocket. I led him to...well...I didn't talk to him like I was supposed to...but he got into her."

"She's not a good person, Od."

"She was nice to me."

"Yeah, for some reason...it would have been better if she was mean. She wanted something from you. Maybe she...took..." he trailed off. Looking like he was struggling with saying something.

"What does she do that is so bad?"

"She's my mom, man. I'm not a tattletale."

"If I was, or am, at risk—I need to know. That's not tattling. I learned a lot form her. I want to talk to her some more."

Loney-Ed grabbed his head. He squeezed his eyes shut. "Can you give me some more Tylenol?"

"They need time to work, it hasn't been long enough," Od said, but still dug in her pack for the bottle, opened it and popped two more out for him. She looked over at him with his face all scrunched up and then popped out another two on top of that.

"Here," Od said and handed him the pills and the Shasta Cola. Loney-Ed took them in one swallow.

"Od...she steals parts of souls."

"What! How?"

"I think she uses the computers to do it. With needles."

"That's how she hooked me up!"

"Yup."

Od tried to focus. There was too much. She just needed to pull everything out of her head, and only put the stuff that mattered now back in. It didn't matter right now that Mrs. Scrobe might have taken part of her soul. She had to save Ed. She was so close. "Let's do this." She grabbed the scarebox, opened the driver's side door, and walked toward the mausoleum.

"Od!" Loney-Ed yelled after her.

She spun around. "What?"

"Emily, er, Ed needs help with her, er, his seat belt," Bernie yelled.

"Then help her, er him...Help them out of the car." She turned back around and started walking again. They would have to follow. Just march and they would. They would have to.

"Od!"

"What?" She spun back around again.

"Uh.." Loney-Ed said. "The mausoleum is...uh...just don't be so..." he fumbled with how to say something again.

"Just spit it out, Lone!"

"You're going to need a heck of a lot more Vicks in your nose."

Od sure wished she would have listened to him.

THE MAUSOLEUM, Devotion, was ruined in death. Splashes. Bodies. Chunks. Ashes. It was heavy with it. There was that word again. *Heavy.* It stung Od's eyes and stuck in her spit as she tried to swallow it back down. Once administered, the Vicks helped, but the stain of old death still painted Devotion's white marble black.

Loney's body lay on the ground with its eyes closed, but it did have a heartbeat, a slow breath, and was still warm. This could work. She had Loney-Ed sit next to Loney's body and they put Ed-Emily just next to them. Standing. Ed-Emily was still looking a bit bewildered, staring around the room and not taking direction very well. She thought that being in a body so old and with so little physical muscles and brain left intact must make working Emily difficult. It might even be hard to hear, think, or see. How scary must it have been for Ed? This was all her fault. She was the one who had gotten the box out and opened it, and she was the one who had wiped his soul from his body. *It's OK*, she told herself. She was going to put everything back. Od tried to remember exactly how far away she was sitting from Ed when she opened the scarebox earlier and sat there, trying her best not to get any of the floor-death on her. Bernie was behind her. Outside. Looking in the window with those big eyes. He was probably trying to hone his powers in case something went wrong. She sighed. Lies ruined everyone.

On the count of three, Od said in her head. Loney-Ed was

paying attention, but his head was in his hands. He nodded. Sniffed. She thought that he might be crying. The headache must have been a migraine. She knew what that was like. She felt bad for him.

One. Loney's body heaved with a breath. Loney-Ed's head rest in his hands. Ed-Emily stood, staring at something above.

Two. Ed-Emily looked around, found Od with their gaze. Od felt the smooth brass button with her fingers. Set in the black wood. Black like the death in the room. The button didn't fit in there. The metal rubbed the wood wrong.

Three. The button. Her fingers.

Four. Something was missing.

Five. It didn't matter. It was time to save Ed. Od pressed the button and the scarebox opened once again.

22

COMPLICATIONS

LONEY'S HEAD THUNDERED. His eyes watered. It hurt so bad. He couldn't think. *Just stare down.* He went back and forth from squeezing his eyes as hard as he could to staring at the lines in the floor close up. A speck of dirt. A bug crawling, trying to pick the speck up. He pressed on the top of his head as hard as he could. It gave a tiny bit of relief, but when he let up, it hurt worse. Then real relief hit as he felt his soul being pushed out of the body he was in. It was a shifting feeling, like his conscious was falling out of the back of him. His hands and arms slipped out of Ed's as if they were sleeves, his torso and legs like a snowsuit, and his head like a Halloween mask. He slipped out of his headache and relief washed his soul.

As soon as he fell from Ed's body, a dirty whiteness poured into the mausoleum. Loney had read about the Pale. It even had its own comic. He tried to focus out of it; on the waking world, or at least on the mausoleum, something concrete, not as vague as real life. It was good practice if ever he had to do this again, since the Pale was thin here. Not much of a blanket covered the marble, mainly just wisps and clumps floating about, but all the living had faded away, including his own body. The only thing that was here that was in the waking world was the scarebox, and it was *raging*. A torrential darkness screamed from it, still pushing against him. He tried to focus harder so he could find his body. He felt a vague draw from something that he suspected was his body, but he needed to make sure. *Focus, Loney, Focus.* Just as his body faded into view below him Emily Cline's body faded in as well. Her body still had a soul in her...no...he could see more than one. The scarebox's blackness was storming against Emily Cline, harder and harder. TWO souls shot out of her, one right after the other...but then there were more. A third soul came out. A fourth. But more, there were even more. Five, six, Loney counted. And they swam into Devotion with abandon. Seven, eight...nine in all! Emily Cline faded away, void of souls. Loney stared at the souls flying around the mausoleum. Some swimming in the heavy air. Some whipping back and forth in violent jerks. Loney looked down at his body and reached for it. It was drawing him in.

OD CLOSED THE BOX. *Nothing had happened.* She watched Loney-Ed, Loney's body, and Ed-Emily the entire time with the box on her lap. They just stood, or lay, or sat where they were.

Loney groaned and opened his eyes. "Headache's gone."

Ed was standing, blinking his eyes. "Ed!" Od got up and ran to her brother. He looked down at her, void of expression. "Ed?" He turned away, looking around at the mausoleum. "Loney...I don't think it worked."

Loney got up. He was looking around the room. Up at the skylights, at the walls, and the empty space high up between them. "Od...I don't think Ed was in Emily," he said. Od looked at Emily Cline. She was still standing. Looking around as well.

"Ed?" Emily looked at her, so did Ed's Body. *What the hell was going on?* "What happened? Loney, did you see what happened?"

"...yeah."

Bernie started screaming from outside.

Od swung around. A body in one of the caskets was getting up. He was mostly rotted, face completely black from mold, rimmed with a pale white. As he dragged himself out of his casket Od noticed that that was not what Bernie was screaming at. There was another half-body that had crawled to the door Bernie was standing at, smearing itself against the glass. Most of its face was gone, including its lips and cheeks, which exposed the full length of its teeth, and gave it a permanent snarl. Another decomposed man was standing, missing all of his leg flesh, somehow managing to walk without most of his muscles. A woman was climbing out of a coffin, withered, wrinkled and tight, but still slack somehow, and moldy. The black slop on the floor that had once been a person was collecting itself and moving. Every dead thing in the room was coming to life, and just when Od thought that the terror inside her could not grow any more they all started coming for her.

The moans and rasps started as they inched toward her. She stepped backward and tripped over an urn. The urn broke open and the ash inside spilled across the floor. She slipped in it, trying to get up, and a skeletal hand with old chunks of wet rot still clinging to it grabbed her from behind. She tried to pull away but couldn't. It dug into her arm, the points of its finger bones closing sharp against her skin. Another hand grabbed her other shoulder. A bloated, spotted, suited man towered over her. She started breathing quick, unable to pull a full breath, trembling in her limbs and chin. Coherent thoughts fled her mind, replaced with an unthinking, empty horror. She couldn't pull away. The finger bones clamped, squeezing harder. That uncontrollable sob that only really little kids fall into began to take her over. Then she felt the first hand come away. A boy stood there. Loney…yeah, Loney was his name…Loney got the hand away, ripped it right from her arm and then pushed himself between her and the other sharp skeleton hand. Her arm felt hot. Loney was pushing her. Those dead faces were looking at her. People in their various stages of rot were walking, crawling, clawing, oozing toward her. Loney was pushing her. So many of them. "Run, Od!" And she did, to the closest door. Opened it and threw herself outside. Loney followed close behind.

She tried to catch her breath, to figure out what was going on. She was still shaking, but as the minutes passed her mind became sharper. She had just closed the box and they started coming to life and attacking her, not like Ed would have...*Ed!* Od went back to the glass door. It was a mess in there. Everything was writhing and shuddering. Rotten guts and human remains in a sick parade. She couldn't see Ed's Body though. "Where is Ed?"

"I don't know." Loney was beside her pressed against the glass. Od searched for Ed, but couldn't see him anywhere. *Maybe from the other side...*As she ran around the mausoleum the rain started. She got to the other side and looked in. It was pretty much the same. The things were just marching around, searching, wandering. "Where is he?"

Loney didn't answer.

"We need his body to put his soul in. What if they're tearing at him like they were tearing at me? Is he on the floor?" Her arm burned. She looked down at it and saw that where the skeletal hand had grabbed her was a thick gash. Some of the hand must have sloughed off, because globs of the dark matter were stuck there, getting in her wound, mixing with her blood. She slapped at it and rubbed it on the side of her shirt. She was going to have to go back into the mausoleum.

"He's right there," Loney said. She couldn't see him though. Not behind a casket or mobbed by the dead. And it didn't look like any of them were feasting on him...Od turned to Loney and he pointed. Opposite the mausoleum, in the grass was Ed's

Body...sitting with a little girl. Od didn't recognize her at first from the back, but then it was obvious. It was Emily Cline. As she got closer, she saw that they weren't only sitting side by side among the newer graves, but they were also holding hands.

"What the hell?"

"I have no idea."

"What are they doing?"

They all looked at them. The two bodies looked content.

"Nine souls came out of Emily's body," said Loney.

"Nine? Why? How? I don't get it."

"It's my mom. She did it."

"Is that why the dead are rising? It's all those souls going into the bodies?"

"Yes."

"Why were they attacking me? How did they get in her? Oh no... is Ed in one of those bodies? One of those rotted bodies? Or in one of those piles of sludge... oh god... was that him trying to grab on to me...was he trying to talk to me...get me to help?"

For a fraction of a second Loney looked at her with widened eyes, as if he hadn't considered it, but then the look was gone and he said, "I didn't see him."

"How would you be able to recognize him?"

"These souls that came out of Emily weren't natural...they were darker. I think they might have been… homemade."

"Homemade?"

Loney stared at the ground for a good full three seconds. Then he took a deep breath and looked into Od's eyes. "I think my mom makes souls."

"*Makes* souls?"

"Yeah. I think she has dozens of them stored on a hard drive she calls a soul box."

"*Dozens*??" Od screamed. "That's what she had me hooked

up to."

"I think she used you as a conduit or something to put the souls into Emily."

"Why?"

"She has to put them somewhere. She makes them and keeps screwing them up. She can't just throw them away, and if she let them run around the house I don't know what would happen. Probably something bad. There used to be a lot of people that would come to the house and I think she was hooking the souls onto those people without them knowing. And now that nobody really comes over I think she has been putting them in houses around town. Basically dumping them where she can."

"Why would somebody want to make a soul?" Od squinted. "How could you even do it?"

"I'm not sure how, exactly...I think she cuts parts of people's souls off and uses those as like a canvas or base or something."

"Your mom steals people's souls, and like, chops them up to make new ones?"

"I told you not to go talk to her."

The rain was falling a bit harder and Bernie came around the corner. She had completely forgotten about him. "Hey guys, I was...what the hell?" Bernie had caught sight of Ed's Body and Emily Cline holding hands in the grass.

"Loney, how do we fix this?" Od asked, pointing the mausoleum. Inside of Devotion, a group of dripping undead scraped and licked at the windows trying to get at them.

"Fuck if I know." Loney rubbed the back of his neck. "I guess we could scare them all out of their bodies…"

"These are screwed-up souls?"

"Yeah, ones that are missing key components that normal souls have… I think they are too aggressive... I don't think that they're going to want to leave those bodies, and if they get scared out they'll probably just go back in. Or they might look for better bodies to inhabit. Maybe ones that already have souls in them. Maybe like us. They have never had a physical life. They were made and screwed up, then dumped into a computer." Loney got lost for a second. Spacing out into Devotion.

"Could you just keep opening the box over and over again? Maybe they will be scared of the bodies and stay out? You know, like the comic says." Bernie said.

"They're different. I'm not sure the same rules would apply," Loney said. "And I don't want one of those things trying to get into me. Especially since my soul already seems to be trying to escape. Plus…I would be cautious about using the scarebox too many times." Od exchanged looks with Loney.

"It might work…"

"You want to go in there and try, Bernie?"

He didn't respond.

Od looked at the creatures in the mausoleum that didn't quite have the facilities, knowledge, or brainpower to open the door. "I feel sorry for them."

"Yeah."

"What if we just went home and then went back to bed?" Bernie suggested.

"Bernie."

"What? Somebody would find them today or whenever and then they would have to deal with them. They probably would just cover it up so nobody got scared. I mean they can't just put that in the paper, right? And if they did, which they wouldn't because, I mean, something like this must have happened sometime in the past and I've never heard of it before…what was I saying? Oh yeah, even if they did we might actually get a newspaper worth reading. People would know a new truth. It would be a service to the community." There was *a* logic to what Bernie was saying.

Od said, "We should go back."

"What?"

"To your home, Loney. And find out what to do from your mom. I don't think we should scare them out again, at least not until we have semi-concrete knowledge."

"What about Ed and his new girlfriend?" Bernie said.

"I wonder why they're holding hands," asked Loney.

"Really," Od said.

"More importantly…why is *she* still moving? She *is* still moving, right? Is there a soul in her or what?" said Loney.

They all walked over to face Ed's Body and Emily Cline. The two looked up at them, and then they all just stared at each other. The rain fell. And they all just stared.

"Well, she's still moving."

"Is Ed in the dead girl?"

"No."

"He wouldn't be holding hands with himself."

"Maybe he would."

"No."

"It's like she's the same as Ed. No soul…but still living…"

They all stared a bit more.

"We're all going to get sick," said Bernie underneath his hoodie. "Let's at least go sit in the car."

"What about Ed's Body?" Od said.

The rain steamed off of Ed as it hit him.

"Let's just take it with us," said Bernie.

"I tried to move it before. It kind of kicked my ass. That was the whole reason for her."

"Well, maybe if we can get her to follow us into the car, Ed's Body will come too," said Bernie.

"And how would we do that?"

Bernie scrunched up his face and sighed. Then he pulled his

hand into the sleeve of his hoodie and grabbed Emily Cline's free hand with it. He curled his lip with his tongue slightly out and fake-gagged as he pulled on her arm. She got up. Then Ed got up. Bernie led them around the mausoleum and Od ran ahead. She opened the door and pulled the seat forward and then Bernie, Emily Cline, and Ed's Body all got into the back seat holding hands. She shut the door behind them and shook her head at Loney, who returned the head shake with a little laugh. Loney got in the passenger side and Od got into the driver's seat. She turned on the car and turned up the heater.

"So, now what?" Bernie said.

"Now we go to Loney's and ask his mom how to fix everything."

"*She* did this," Loney said.

"I know. So that means that she probably knows how to fix it."

"She's not going to fix it."

"Well, I don't know how to fix them," Od gestured to the back seat. "Or *them*." She gestured to the mausoleum. "Now daylight is coming and my parents are coming home soon..."

"I don't..." Loney trailed off, abandoning whatever he was going to say.

Od sighed. "What if we could...wait, where's Ed?"

They were all silent.

"Where's Ed?"

Bernie said, "Uh...he's right here." Od glared at him through the rearview mirror. "Oh, you mean *Ed* Ed." Od started to say something back, but remembered something. She gasped and grabbed her backpack.

"I'd guess that he's probably still in the pocket in your house," said Loney.

Od unzipped the pack and reached inside, pushing things

around until she found the action figure. She brought it up to her face. "Ed?" The thing remained still. "Ed?"

Bernie and Loney exchanged looks.

"Ed, if you're in there, please move…anything." She put the figure into a sitting position on the dashboard and stared intently at it, waiting for the slightest of movement from the plastic toy.

Bernie looked from Od to Loney and made the sign for crazy. Loney frowned but looked unsure.

"Oh shut up, guys—you don't know everything." She shook her head. "So we're going to my house. Since Ed isn't here or in this…" The word for the toy escaped her for a second.

"Dengar," Bernie said.

"What?"

"That's Dengar, the bounty hunter."

Od rolled her eyes. "Since he's not in Dengar, the bounty hunter, he's probably in the house and we can put Ed right into Ed's body."

She put the car into gear and pulled out onto the road. It was raining even harder now and the windshield wipers were having a hard time keeping up even on the highest setting. Ed's Body and Emily Cline were still holding hands. Bernie was squished as far as he could toward the door away from Emily. Loney re-started the mixtape they had found earlier. It played Tiffany's cover of "I Think We're Alone Now."

"I didn't know that being in an action figure was even an option," said Bernie. To which Od and Loney didn't respond. "Did you guys ever see *Dawn of the Dead*?" Bernie asked.

Nobody said anything.

"It was really good."

Nobody said anything.

"Super scary."

Still, nobody replied.

"And gross."

WHEN THEY GOT BACK TO N, Od parked on the side furthest from Bob's again and they all went inside. Od made Bernie pull Emily and Ed through each room of the house, one by one, where Od would declare that Ed's body was here and Ed should come home. Her wording felt a little eyeroll-worthy, but honesty could feel that way sometimes. Then they went into the kitchen again, sat and waited for about thirty minutes.

"It's still not working."

"…maybe Ed isn't here," said Loney.

"Where would he be?"

Loney didn't say anything.

"We're going to your house," Od told Loney. "Bernie, you stay here with Ed's Body and Emily, in case Ed shows up and decides to get back into his body."

"Od... I don't think this is a good idea."

"I don't have any others. My parents are coming home and it's starting to get light outside. My brother could be being tortured in some way, or trapped somewhere, or I don't *know* what."

"Then let's have some sort of plan."

The doorbell rang. Everyone stopped and looked at each other, including Ed's Body and Emily Cline. "Who is that?" said Bernie.

"If we go into my room we can see who's at the front door." Loney and Od and Bernie left Ed's Body and Emily in the kitchen and went into Od's room. Walt Disney and Steve Martin were extremely excited to see them and jumped up on all of them, trying to lick their faces and sniff them to death. Od motioned for everybody to get down and then she led them, crawling, to the big window that faced the front of the house, as the dogs made sure everyone had an even amount of dog spit distributed on each of their faces. They all rose to a crouch once they were beside the dressers and looked out at the doorbell-ringers. There were four of them standing at the front door. In the dark, Od couldn't tell who they were.

Until Loney said, "Damn."

"Who is it?" Bernie asked.

"It's my brothers." It was the Scrobe boys. All of them. At Od's door. She didn't even know that they knew where she lived. She didn't like it.

"Why?" she said.

"I don't know."

The doorbell rang again.

"What should we do?" Od said.

"Let's pretend we're not here," Bernie said.

A loud crash came from the kitchen. "I think Ed and Emily just blew our cover."

"They won't go away. They must know your parents are gone. If we don't answer, they will try and get in." Loney had a serious look on his face.

"Well, let's open the door then," Od said.

"No!" Bernie said.

"Why not? What the hell are they going to do?"

"It's the Scrobes, Od! They are..." Bernie said. He looked at Loney. "No offense, but..." He looked at Od. "They kill things and they smell weird. Their parents don't care. I've heard some crazy stuff that they did and I believe most of it. And they got away with it all." Bernie looked at Loney again. "No offense."

Loney and Od looked at each other. "He's not necessarily wrong, Od. I don't even like them. You know what Gatch did. That isn't even half of it."

"I'm not afraid of them," Od said, and she wasn't... Not even of Gatch. *Creepy little fucker.* "Let's open the door." Her heart beat hard in her ears. She balled her hands into fists because they started to shake for some reason.

"Why don't I go out the front and tell them something about why you're not here," Loney said. "...like, you're in the graveyard or at a friend's house. Then you can sneak out the back and go..." Loney stopped and sighed. Almost as if he didn't agree with what he was thinking about saying next.

"...talk to your mom."

"She'll probably respond better to you, anyway. It's not a good idea. But it is *an* idea. And if we want Ed back... I can't figure it out. Everything I've tried to do has ended in switched bodies or the dead rising from their grave. If you think you can get her to talk to you and tell you what to do then do it. I don't trust her with you, but I trust her more than I do my brothers." So did she. "Just don't let her hook you up to that thing again. You need *all* of your soul Od, no matter what anyone says." Loney looked into her eyes. "*That* I am sure of."

Od said, "What are you going to tell them?"

"Maybe that you went to Katie's house."

"Katie Cooper?"

"Yeah, you guys are friends, right?"

"Yeah."

"She would help you out and she used to be into the macabre. It kinda fits."

"Yeah."

"So, you're at her house."

"What if they go over there?"

"Her parents are home, I take it. I doubt they'll do that. I would say you were at the graveyard, but I don't want them going there. Who knows what they would do if they found Devotion."

"So meet you back here?"

"Yeah."

"Good luck."

"Good luck."

They looked at each other.

"What am I doing?" Bernie said.

"You are staying here and making sure that Ed's Body is all right and that the dogs don't eat Emily."

"…OK. Corpse Wrangler, got it."

Loney looked back at Od. "Hey…we uh…got Ed's Body back here…"

"And..?" Od asked. But she knew.

"…nothing…" Loney said.

She kissed him on the lips for five seconds. Eyes closed. She didn't think of Short Round.

23

JENNY

JENNY SCROBE GATHERED the needles Odlyn had pulled out of her neck and started separating the wires. She put the needles back in their box according to size, then coiled the wires and set them aside as well. She ejected N's disk from the drive and called, "Gatch!"

Jenny had been making souls for nearly twenty years now and had botched a good deal of them, especially in the beginning. That wouldn't have been a huge problem, except for that you couldn't really throw souls away. So when you made one that was too *this* or too *that*, missing this, having too much of that, you were stuck with them. Then you had to find places to put them. Homemade souls acted as a sort of pollutant if simply left where they were created, which is what she did at first, and if they were discarded, whether it was to any part the waking world, or in the general Pale, they caused *bad* things to happen.

In the beginning she made very simple souls. So when she made errors she could put them in random pockets or occasionally lock them into mirrors when the situation presented itself. As she got better at the process though it got a bit more difficult to place the flawed attempts, since they were more complex. She ultimately had to find stronger houses in town to put them in or attach them to people. Attaching them was tricky, but she was good at tricky. When people stopped visiting her that option dried up, and she couldn't very well attach the souls by phone, even though she did try a few times. When Jenny got her technique down and she was making really complex things, souls with nuance and a detailed structure, with a roundness that wasn't present before, she had to find quasi-permanent homes for them. She found that she couldn't lock them in pockets or mirrors or what-have-you reliably anymore, but there just weren't many options available, and their creation was a necessary step, so other options were created. When she finally started making souls that were so intricate that they could pass for natural ones, souls that began to possess something she could not quantify or define, she decided that she needed to give them at least a shot at life. So she started having kids.

All of her kids were weak when they were first born, so it was easy to strangle the natural souls out of them and put her true children into the empty vessels. Natural souls passed all the time, so there was no reason to worry about them; they would simply go where they would go next, or not go anywhere, or simply end. She didn't give it much thought, because a beginning or an ending was just something that happened. No matter what she did, or didn't do, both a beginning and an ending would happen for them. It was just a matter of when. She had not made those souls, but she had made the babies, so why not put the souls she made into those babies. It would make them her true children and it would truly be creating life, from the very inside to the very out.

Jenny had quite a few souls left over that she still had to find homes for, ones that weren't intricate enough for waking life. Some were a bit too aggressive or simple, others too much this, and others not enough that. So when Odlyn came to her with her problem, and a direct line to a house like N, Jenny first saw the opportunity to dump them into its pocket. But when Jenny got a look at Od's soul she got another idea. Odlyn's soul was so odd.

So interesting…so…thorough…it was a work of art, really…and there was so much of it. So she sliced some of it off. Odlyn wouldn't miss it. And the things that Jenny could do with it…well, it could raise everything to an entirely new level. She could use it to make a soul so much like a natural one it would make the most intricate soul she had made so far look like one of her screw-ups. In fact, she might be able to make a soul *better* than a natural one. The thought made the hairs on the back of her neck stand up.

Jenny typed something into the computer. "Gatch!" Where was he? He was at the same time Jenny's worst and best attempt at a soul and child. That soul she made fit so nicely in the body she birthed, so unlike Loney. Loney's natural soul wouldn't leave. She thought that she had wrung it out of him and promptly tried to replace it with one of her more intricate souls, but apparently the kid's natural soul was still there. She didn't know this, so when the soul she had made wouldn't go in, she forced it and the two fused. When she realized what had happened she tried to separate them, and push the natural one out, but it was too late. She was never really sure how much of what remained in Loney was natural and how much was what she had made, but the soul hybrid that remained inside his body was so loose that it often wandered when Loney slept. When he was really tiny and they went to the cemetery for a relative's funeral, the thing tried to leave his body completely. It was subconsciously mesmerized by the soulless bodies for some reason, though Loney himself wasn't consciously aware of it. She got him out of there as quickly as she could and used a little trick—she was good at tricks—to keep his soul put for the time being. She doubted whether Odlyn was telling the truth about him not being in the graveyard. She would find out soon though, and bad things would happen if the girl were lying. "Gatch!" Where was that boy?

24

FAILURE

ED FLOWED THROUGH THE TUNNEL that he had mistaken as a doorway to inhabit the dead girl in his kitchen. Now he found himself back in the church, tied to the cross with the other souls. He was still unable to get free from the cross, but now that he had found the tunnels, it didn't really matter. The way to get free wasn't outward. It wasn't to try to break the bonds that held him. It was *inward*. To use the souls and mirrors and ponds and reflections together. To use the tunnels they made. He was sure that they could take him to many different places if used correctly, places the souls on the cross had been before, just as they had taken him to his house, where he had lived what felt like another life with Aureolin. They could also force you into bits of life that the imprisoned souls had been connected to…and they might be able to do much more.

Ed looked down into the church, out from the cross of souls. The Are were together again, maybe using their souls the same way he used the souls and tunnels here, living lives that were long gone, or projecting themselves into places around town. He looked toward the spot where he had let the tiny soul get burned away. He was so sure in the moment that he was right, that he was liberating the soul, releasing it into the next life, to Heaven, or some sort of afterlife or rebirth, but he had been wrong. And it cost not only a life, but the soul of someone he didn't even know. It was worse than murder. He didn't deserve to use the tunnels. He didn't deserve to be. He looked down at the base of the cross. There was the stone that had fallen after the little soul had burned away. It was a bright, pure light. He found himself drawn to it and could feel all the other souls that were stuck to the cross with him being pulled toward it as well. If they hadn't been tied to the cross, they would have all been yanked to the stone.

What was that stone? A piece of the soul? Was it the soul's shell? Was it a piece of the light that had burned the thing away? Residue? A chrysalis? No. It was his failure. His trophy for destroying something's eternal essence. He should hang here forever. In despair. In tragedy. He was meant to be crucified. He didn't try for any tunnels. He didn't fall into the mirrors. He just hung.

Until he felt a sharp crack from the outside. A disturbance of hundreds of souls in a sudden moment. A disturbance that was spreading.

25

BARGAINING

OD WENT OUT THE BACK sliding door, cut through Bob's property and ran down Wisner to the Scrobe house. The front door was unlocked and she knew that nobody would answer if she knocked, so she let herself in. She walked down the twisted hallway that hooked right and then back to the left and opened the large door to Mrs. Scrobe's bedroom.

Mrs. Scrobe was on the bed. The TVs were on and both computers were up and running. She looked up from her computer with those old glasses hanging at the tip of her nose.

"So you cut part of my soul off?" Od asked.

Mrs. Scrobe didn't seem surprised to see her at all. She simply took the glasses from her face and set them next to one of the computer monitors. She sighed. "Sit down, Odlyn."

Od walked over to the bed and sat down on that hardwood chair where she had been earlier.

"I did. I clipped a piece of it."

"And you think that's OK?"

"Yes and no. The soul is a complex creature. It is both a whole and parts. There is an extra casing around it that can be clipped. It doesn't serve a purpose. I don't clip all of it, anyway. I clip about half of the casing. Afterward it fills itself in. Granted, it is a bit thinner, but it is still there."

"You think God makes souls with extra parts?"

"Well, I'm not going to get into the whole God thing with you, but as for extra parts...to be perfectly honest it serves as a small purpose of filtering and protection. BUT it is still there after I clip it. And although it is just thinner, it doesn't make it any less strong." Od seriously doubted that, but how could she possibly debate with Mrs. Scrobe about this? She didn't even know what she was talking about.

"Filtering what? Protection from what? Seems like those are pretty important functions."

"They only come into play when the soul is out of the body. Protecting was the wrong word. Anchoring is a better one. The casing limits the bodiless soul. It filters things you perceive, so you don't see the whole thing. And it protects the soul from interaction with the waking world. It gives you this sort of bubble that makes interacting with the waking world much more difficult. It anchors you. If you ask me, a soul after the physical life without a casing is a much freer one." Od thought that there was probably some truth there, but only some. Grains of salt and all that. She was sure that there must be something bad about not having something that was originally attached to your soul though, but once again she couldn't really argue the point.

"What do you use the casing for?"

"I make souls."

"How?"

"That is a long and complicated story."

"Why?"

"Because I can."

"Can you teach me?"

Mrs. Scrobe looked deep into Od. As if she wasn't seeing her the right way before. She frowned. Looked down. Then looked back up at Od again. She started to say something...

"I could be an apprentice."

Mrs. Scrobe just continued to frown at her.

Od waited until she thought Mrs. Scrobe was going to say something again and then added, "You can cut the rest of the casing off of my soul."

Mrs. Scrobe narrowed her eyes, as if she was putting a fine point on her vision to see into Od, her mind, and intentions. She was working it out in her head. Weighing what Od was saying. And then laughing a bit. Od was pretty sure that Mrs. Scrobe knew that she was telling her the truth about both things. She did want to learn how to make a soul, and everything else Mrs. Scrobe knew. And she was ready to have the rest of her soul casing cut off. That is why she thought that Loney's mom was so confused.

"Odlyn, I don't think you can learn to make a soul."

"Why not?"

"Let's not get into that right now. We can talk about that later. Why do you want me to clip your soul again? Planning for a freer afterlife?"

"I need Ed back. It didn't work going into the dream and I think that part of the reason was because you may have had some ulterior motives."

"Why do you say that, sweetie?"

"'Cause a bunch of souls came out of the dead girl that we were supposed to be putting Ed in," Od looked into the perfect green eyes before her. "And not one of them was Ed."

"Hmm. Well, that wasn't my intention. I meant to put them into N's pocket, and it should have worked. I don't know why Ed didn't go into her. You did talk to him, yes?"

"So, you only meant to make our house haunted?"

"Honey, N is full of souls, and other such things. They're stuffed everywhere, all sorts of them." Od wasn't really surprised that there were ghosts in her house. Of course she didn't know that it was a whole bunch of them with 'other such things', 'all sorts', and 'stuffed everywhere', but that didn't matter right now.

"Whatever. I just want to get Ed back, I need some information, and I want to learn to make a soul…if I can…and in exchange you can have the rest of my casing. But you have to do the job right this time and not put anything else into my house."

"Deal."

26

GATCH

GATCH COULD SMELL THE DEATH on Loney as he opened the front door and stepped outside. "What's going on?" Loney asked. Not just one dead thing, but a lot of dead things. Old dead things. It was so sticky. So sweet. Almost too sweet. Almost.

"Where's your girlfriend?" asked Thad.

Loney shut the door behind himself. "Od's going to talk to Mom," said Loney. Which made Corlan laugh. Everything made him laugh.

"Really?" Thad said.

Loney nodded.

"Let's go talk up there." Thad nodded to the trees on the hill behind the black car.

So Corlan, Bray, Thad, and Gatch led Loney up a little hill into a forest that was probably part of the Perfect property. There was a fence that opened to it and a bench just inside. Then beyond that a couple paths led into a thick forest that nobody could see into from the outside. The rain had quieted down a bit and what little was still falling was blocked by the trees. Of course, the trees still did drip a bit on them.

The rain had punched up the smells everywhere. The pine was so strong Gatch was sure everyone else could smell it. The smell of the rain itself was strong too. But there was also the smell of a wet wasp nest nearby. Sage bushes. The dirt. A couple of rabbits somewhere. Gatch could also smell the fear steaming off of his brother, Loney. Gatch hated that smell. It was this musky mildewy dankness that some people just soaked in all the time. It made him hate some people. He didn't smell it so much from his other brothers, but then again, his other brothers rarely smelled like anything. Gatch wished the blonde girl was here. She smelled good, even with that fear musk.

"What's going on?" Loney said.

Thad was the one who normally did the talking. He didn't really have a problem with it like Corlan and Bray did. In fact, Thad *liked* to talk. Corlan could talk, but he mostly just laughed. Bray never said anything, as far as Gatch knew, at least not unless it was absolutely necessary. Gatch could talk pretty well though. He could read pretty well too. Although he wasn't particularly fond of either.

"Mom wanted us to talk to you," said Thad.

"Talk to me?"

"Yeah... Did you go in the graveyard?"

He definitely went into the graveyard. Might have rolled around with some dead bodies too, Gatch thought. He could also smell something else on Loney that he couldn't place, a coldness inside. It was a new smell and it kind of reminded him of the blonde girl, but he didn't know why. There was also some of her on him too now.

Loney looked at Gatch. He knew that Gatch could smell things, but didn't know the extent of it. Their mom had told him that *she* was the one who could smell it all, but Gatch knew that Loney suspected it was him. Gatch smiled at him.

"No."

Thad looked at Gatch. That was his cue. Gatch looked back at him and nodded.

"I knew it!" Loney said to Gatch. "I knew Mom couldn't

smell it. I knew it was you."

"You're not supposed to go in the graveyard."

"I know. But why do you care?"

Their mom didn't tell Loney much. She gave him a lot of the comics with a lot of information in them, but didn't think he could handle everything at once. She told the others though. Not that she just laid it all out for them, but with them she was much more straightforward. If they asked her about something she would answer. Like when Gatch asked about death.

There was a smell when death happened. A complex aroma. As if every smell a person had soaked in over all the years of their life was released at that moment. It was intoxicating. The best smell that there was. And when something died that smell washed over him. Everything in life paled at that smell. It didn't last long, a few moments maybe, but it was everything to him. Then as the deathsmell faded, the sweet smell of the dead set in. The longer someone was dead, the sweeter it got. Until it was too much. So sticky. So rich. Like a cake made completely of frosting. It was a mockery of the deathsmell. Loney had some of that on him now mixing with his fear.

Gatch wasn't allowed to kill anything. Unless his mom said it was OK. She said that it was wrong, especially if it was a person or a big animal. But sometimes when the urge for the smell got to be too much she let him kill *something*. Usually a small animal. Bugs didn't really do it. Sometimes there was a faint whiff of the smell when he squashed them, but not enough to be worth the effort.

Gatch didn't really understand why killing things was wrong. In school, in the higher grades, they said that there was an overpopulation problem on Earth; he heard that straight from a teacher's mouth. He also heard people on TV call humans a 'pair-a-sight' to the Earth. Which was a bug that infested something and made it sick. And his mom told him that souls are stuck in the meatsacks everyone called bodies, and when the person dies the soul goes on afterwards. Of course she didn't say where exactly, and those weren't the words that she used, but to him it sounded like the souls were trapped in meatbags.

Even kids at school and people on TV talked like after your life was over your soul would go to a magic world where everything was bright white and all your good dreams came true. It didn't make sense that everyone clung so desperately to being alive, and it made less sense that they clung to everyone else on the planet to be alive, no matter whether they knew them or not. In their eyes, by their own words, they were all just a knife or a hammer away from every hope that they ever had becoming real. Plus, why would death smell so good if it wasn't supposed to happen? It was something beautiful that everyone shied away from. People even made prisons where they kept people that did bad things there. Nobody wanted to be in prisons, yet they all wanted to stay trapped in meatbags. Gatch didn't get it.

It was Gatch's job to carry the spikes. Three of them. Bray was supposed to grab Loney's legs and hold on. He was the fastest of the brothers. He didn't talk, but he could move like lightning. Like a small animal in danger. Like a car. So quick. Then Corlan, since he was the strongest and the biggest, would get him by the shoulders or something and hold onto him. Thad had the gun. He was the one who was supposed to shoot Loney. Once they confirmed that he had been in the graveyard, that was when they were supposed to do it. So when he smelled the death on Loney, he got the spikes ready in his hands behind his back. He thumbed the points and pressed until he could smell his own blood. He'd get in trouble for that. He always did.

Bray moved from where he was standing to Loney's ankles before anyone could see. Loney was surprised; he stumbled, tripped over the back of his own heels and fell to the ground backward. He let out a scream of pain when he hit. It looked like he might have hit a rock. Corlan lumbered over and grabbed Loney around the shoulders, but Loney was thrashing, putting up a much better fight than Gatch thought he could have. Then Corlan pinned Loney to the ground with his knees in his shoulders. Loney screamed again and Corlan covered his mouth with his hands. Thad came around Corlan to face Loney and pulled out the gun with his left hand.

"Mom, says we have to." He knelt down to Loney, whose eyes were wide. And although they didn't really show it, for a second, Gatch could smell the tears welling up. Kind of like the ocean. Gatch thought that Loney was going to start crying, but his eyes only filled up with tears, and when he blinked them away, no more replaced them. Thad brought the gun down to Loney's neck. A homemade gun with a groove on the top of it. Gatch handed one of the spikes to Thad, who clicked it into the top of the gun's barrel and shot it into Loney's neck. Thad had said that he would carry the spikes, but then what was Gatch supposed to do—just stand there smelling it all? He wanted to help. He wanted to carry the spikes. They gave off a buzz that went into his fingers and hands, up to his wrists even. He liked them. Gatch handed Thad another, which Thad shot into Loney's neck just next to the other. The final one Thad put into his chest. Loney screamed underneath Corlan's hand when each spike was driven in. There wasn't much blood, just a few drops that his brothers didn't bother wiping away. Blood always made death smell better. It was such a perfect complement to that round landscape of smell that erupted from somebody when they died. This electric body smell. Violent death always smelled the best. Gatch used to go to the hospital and sneak around, hoping to catch the deathsmell in the ER or the hallways, but the deaths there didn't smell as good as the violent ones, and he wasn't received very well there. Then when he tried to be honest and explain why he was there, he got in a lot of trouble.

Corlan got off of Loney and took his hands off of his mouth. Loney's eyes looked heavy, swimming in a new well of unshed tears. The spikes didn't kill him, of course. They weren't supposed to kill him.

"There," said Thad. "Now you can go have fun with your girlfriend in the graveyard and your soul won't leave. We fixed it." Loney looked tired, but he got up. He was standing kind of loppy like his body wasn't working quite up to speed. He managed to put his head up though, and spit a nice size loogie onto Thad's shirt. It smelled like acid, vomit, soda, and something salty. "You're welcome," said Thad. Loney rocked back and forth and then lunged at Thad. He missed him, fell about two feet short actually, landing on the ground with a dull thud and a tiny groan. Corlan laughed. And that is where they all left him, lying in the woods. Before they got too far away Thad turned back and said, "Don't try and take them out. It'll hurt a lot. We'll put more in if you do. Five of them. Plus they're keeping your soul in your body, stupid."

They all turned to go back down to the Perfect property and then to the street. Gatch felt really weird. He had just helped his brother, Loney. He had never really done that before. It actually felt pretty good. *Weird.*

27

GOGGLES AND GAUNTLETS

THE SCROBES DID HAVE A BASEMENT, which was a strange thing in Northern California, and it smelled like electricity down there. When Od asked Mrs. Scrobe why she had lied about having one before, she just ignored the question and sent Od down there to get a suitcase. She tried her best to ignore what she had imagined about the basement earlier. She also tried not to look at all the strange things down there and focus on trying to find the case, but it proved difficult. There weren't any limbless girls down there bearing children, tied down or otherwise. Instead, the basement was filled with large constructions of metal and wood with wires laced around their supports.

The constructions reached all the way to the ceiling and overran the room. There was no order to how they were laid out that Od could see, but Mrs. Scrobe had given her directions to the dank maze. She wrote them down on a scrap of paper and drew a quick little map that was impossibly detailed considering the time she took to draw it. It even had a key that told what the little symbols on the map meant. *Right, right, left, right*, Od thought as she followed the dotted arrow line on the map. Mrs. Scrobe said that when she got to the right place she would see a shelving unit made of dark wood. On the bottom of it would be four metal cylinders and behind those would be the suitcase. She was not to disturb the metal cylinders.

There was so much stuff down there. So much *strange* stuff. Most of it was packed in cardboard boxes or big canvas bags, but the things that weren't covered up were fascinating. There were five identical statues of a bird-lizard thing, a giant mirror of black glass that Od could barely see her own reflection in, a beautifully broken-in red leather saddle too small for an adult, and a cache of what must have been over twenty swords. The smell of electricity ran through the basement like veins, but in some parts it smelled like a hardware store, and in others a used bookstore. There was also a low constant hum that followed her wherever she went down there. It was a crackling hum, though she didn't think many people would have noticed the crackling part. She could have spent a long time exploring the place, but that wasn't a thought for her right now. Not a prominent thought anyway. Right now she just needed the suitcase.

It was brown and yellow, leather and canvas. The type you'd find in your grandparents' attic. It looked worn, but not thrashed. The zipper was still good and so was the handle. She thought of Emily Cline's coffin as she pulled it off the shelf. She carried it back through the basement maze and dragged it up the steps, then picked it up again as she went through the house and back to Loney's mom's bedroom. It was fairly heavy, but she only had to switch hands once. When she brought it in and laid it on the bed, Mrs. Scrobe smiled and unlatched it.

"Now, these things are a bit quirky," Mrs. Scrobe said as she opened the suitcase.

Inside, the case was filled to the brim with red and black yarn. It wasn't wrapped or bundled in the slightest, just stuffed in like packing Styrofoam—ghost poops, as Od's mom called them. Mrs. Scrobe's eyes lit up as she pulled the skinny black and crimson snakes from the suitcase and revealed what was beneath: a pair of gloves...or...*what was it that the knights would wear into battle on their hands?*

Like everything in the Scrobe house, the gloves looked like they had been built there. They didn't have the smoothness or clean lines of something that had been formed in a factory; they were rough and complicated, constructed of segregated metal pieces. Most of it was a dull steel, but there were a few copper sections as well. There were green boards and black wires underneath those sections, twisting and disappearing from sight. The fabric that held the glove together looked like leather, but when Od finally felt it she knew it was something else. On the back of the…*gauntlets! That's what they were, gauntlets!*…below the fingers were several burnished plates and a housing that contained either a glass container or clear jewel of some sort. Buckles hung loose below.

Next to the gauntlets in the suitcase was a pair of goggles. They were fixed as the gauntlets were, with both steel and copper segments, short wires sprouting and connecting at seemingly random sections. On one side, between the lens and the head strap was a metal housing with two nine-volt batteries. The lenses looked very similar to that mirror with the black glass she had seen in the basement, and their rims were made of a smooth, dark, red wood.

"Quirky like how?"

"Like they don't work very well. They have a mind of their own sometimes and they glitch too much to be reliable." Mrs. Scrobe looked up at Od. "That is why they are in the basement."

Another mess-up, Od thought, and looked down at the metal accessories. "Well, what are they *supposed* to do?"

"They are supposed to give the user contact with dead things, or the bodiless," Mrs. Scrobe was caressing the things—tracing their lines with her fingertips. She looked at them as if she were longing for something or remembering a great-whatever. She kept her head down, but her eyes moved up to Od. It made the greens of her eyes obscured by her brows, two beautiful-sick half-moons setting in an upside down world. Mrs. Scrobe's demeanor changed, and a softness Od hadn't quite appreciated before drained completely out of the woman. "The gloves should be able to touch a soul. The goggles should let you see them." Lightness came back to her voice and her face smoothed again as she lifted her head. "Both run on batteries."

"But I need to know *where* he is," Od said. That was the real problem. As cool as these things were, she didn't see how they could locate Ed when she couldn't even find him in the pocket.

"You don't think he's in the house?"

"I don't know."

"Well, I bet he is. It is a place to start anyway."

Start? Od thought. *Hadn't she begun long ago?* Od picked up the goggles. They were lighter than she thought they'd be. "I'll be able to see his soul with these?"

"Have you ever played *Pac-Man*?"

"Yeah..." Ms. Pac-Man *was a better game though,* Od thought.

"Well, I borrowed the graphic of the ghosts from that to represent souls. So when you look through the goggles, his soul will look like one of those..." Od must have been looking at her strangely because Mrs. Scrobe got defensive. "I was going to change it when I got them working better. I think I might have been able to get a more realistic view of them with some more adding and tweaking..." She looked at the items again with a long distance in her eyes. Was it regret? "But once I started making more important things...it all went to the basement."

"So all of the souls are just going to look like the *Pac-Man* ghosts? How will I be able to tell them apart?"

"Some will be different colors at least."

"How will I be able to tell Ed apart from the other souls?"

"The newer ones, they are brighter...he will be the brightest by a long shot."

"How will the gloves help?"

"Wear them. And when you find Ed, grab him. Push him towards his body or the other dead body, or whatever. He should get the idea and go into it."

"Why didn't we do this before?"

"The other way was simpler. Easier. And it doesn't have glitches. These things," Mrs. Scrobe said as she gestured to the goggles and gauntlets, "are very glitchy. It's possible they don't work well enough for what you need."

Od sighed.

"I have one more thing that can help," Mrs. Scrobe said and she pulled that long, green, needle box out from under a pillow. She thumbed through it and found a very short needle. "This is a Spout, or funnel, if you prefer. If I plug it into you, you can probably hook Ed's soul onto you. Then walk him over to his body. Twist the Spout until the arrows line up and it will lock the soul onto you. Twist it the other way and it will release him."

"And why didn't we do *that* before?"

"Well first off, it's more painful and more uncomfortable than the needles. Second, it is entirely possible that we can't remove it afterwards. Third, hooking a soul onto you is fairly simple, relatively speaking, but getting it out is much harder. Many times they don't want to leave. I know he's your brother and you think that he would do so willingly, but the Pale changes people and being without a body changes a soul." Mrs. Scrobe rolled the Spout in her fingers. "You could theoretically reach inside yourself and grab his soul with the gloves, if he won't or *can't* leave, for whatever reason, but there is no real way to reach inside yourself with the gloves without making a hole...which is a bit messy. Plus you'd have to avoid grabbing your own soul and pulling it out, which might be easy…or near impossible. Long story short…" *Too late.* "…getting a soul stuck inside you is a worse problem then losing it in a pocket." Mrs. Scrobe held the Spout up. "This is a last resort type of thing." Od was beginning to think that last resort type things were a necessity in life.

"How many times have you done this?"

Mrs. Scrobe held up her hand in an OK sign, closed one eye, and looked through it with the other one. It wasn't an OK sign; it was a zero.

"Let's plug it in."

They used the same gun, but with a different fitting on the top. It did hurt, but not as much. It was a hell of a lot more uncomfortable though, and really itchy. And although the spout-needle was short, the sucker was fat.

"Ready for your end of the bargain?" Mrs. Scrobe asked and jangled the box of needles.

"One more thing," Od said. "How would I get a bunch of souls out of dead bodies without the funnel?"

"The nine in the girl?"

"Yeah. They are in other dead bodies now. In the mausoleum."

"Excuse me?"

"How do I get them out?"

"You have made quite a mess, haven't you?"

"*You* made quite a mess. I didn't even know they were there. Now I have to get them out and clean everything up, and I don't even know what to do with them after I get them out."

"Where to put them. That is the question. I've been coming up with creative solutions for that for a while. None are right though, I think. There was a little bit of room left in N, though. You can put them in there."

"So we can't just let them go? Like to just float away to another house, or haunt the graveyard, or to an afterlife?"

"That is a big no. Bad things happen when you do that."

"Like what?"

"That is too complicated an idea to discuss at the moment, one I don't fully understand either. Put them in N's pocket."

Od chewed her cheek. "How do I get them there?"

"Use the Spout. Hook them within you. Walk them over to your house and then release them into…no, bring them here…no, forget it. Leave them where they are. I'll deal with it."

"And you're sure we can't just scare them out or whatever and let them go?"

Something flashed on Mrs. Scrobe's face. Fear. It looked wrong there, so it fled almost immediately. "I will only say it one more time. Bad things would happen if you do that. *Bad* things."

"What? Why?"

"Just forget about the ones in the mausoleum. I'll deal with it."

"How?"

"Never you mind!" It was a look that said, *don't you dare ask another question on the subject.* Od shut up. "Now how about that soul of yours?"

"OK, what do I do?"

"Grab that cardboard box from under the bed and we'll get this done quick."

Od looked under the bed and found the box, but as she pulled it out a board from something, that must have been loose, twisted. A bunch of small metal cubes, that looked just like the hard drive Mrs. Scrobe called the 'soul box', came tumbling to the floor. Loney had said she kept souls in there, *dozens* of them in one box, and Od was staring at too many boxes to count. She gasped. Had Mrs. Scrobe made hundreds, maybe *thousands* of souls, only to keep them in boxes under her bed?

Od came back up to the bed with the cardboard box Mrs. Scrobe needed and she began to sort things from it. Od got the pills from the dresser again, where one of the Scrobe boys must have put them back. She held them in her hand. *Twelve more*, she thought. *She would probably want me to take twelve more.* There were fifty, maybe a hundred, left in the bottle. She imagined the hundred multiplied over and over again. She looked away from the pills and at the bed. Possibly thousands of souls were under that bed, all stuffed into little boxes, never to see the real world.

Od stared at the corner of the needle box. Its green covering and beige stitching came together in a point there. The stitching was coming loose. A string was coming undone. Frayed. It was, as all strings were, made from other tinier ones…one string was actually many smaller strings. Od grabbed the pill bottle and opened it. She dumped a fistful into her hand and jumped onto the bed. She pinned Mrs. Scrobe's arms down with her knees and shoved the pills into her mouth. She shut her mouth forcefully with one hand and plugged her nose with the other. She held her there as the large woman thrashed her head back and forth. Od could feel her teeth crunching up the pills as she tried to get her mouth open for some air, but Od wouldn't let her. Eventually Mrs. Scrobe swallowed and crunched and swallowed again and Od let go of her mouth and fell off her. She threw the gauntlets and the goggles into the suitcase, then dove under the bed and grabbed as many of the soul boxes as she could carry. Mrs. Scrobe screamed above her, swinging from side to side. The bed creaked. Her voice was a guttural wrench. A low throaty scream with high pitches squeaking into it. The sounds somebody makes when nothing else matters, when they are faced with something they can't imagine. The bed shifted and just as Od rolled out from under it, it collapsed. Od had gotten three of the boxes out and went to throw them into the suitcase, but Mrs. Scrobe somehow had her by the wrist. The meaty grip enveloped half her forearm. It was strong and Od could feel it cutting off the circulation from her hand, forcing her to drop the two boxes it held. The other box fell into the suitcase.

Mrs. Scrobe was still screaming. No words. Just this horrid, primal sound. She was clawing to get up. Her massive frame was now half on the floor and half on the bed, and she was using Od's arm to steady herself. The weight was incredible. And Od couldn't handle it. She found Mrs. Scrobe's thumb and pried at her fingers, but they wouldn't release. She stretched away from her, but Mrs. Scrobe was beginning to stand. If the woman took one step she would be close enough to grab the rest of Od, to crush her, or whatever she had in mind. If anything was even in the screaming woman's mind at the moment.

Od reached for something, anything. She felt the bed, the covers, and came up with the green box. She gripped it at the frayed corner and swung it hard with her free hand at Mrs. Scrobe. As it made contact, the needles exploded from the box. A shower of silver and gold lines spinning and falling and sticking into Mrs. Scrobe at all angles. In her face and breasts. Her arms and shoulders. One particularly thin needle glinted in the blue glow of the TVs as it stood crookedly from of Mrs. Scrobe's eyelid, pinning it halfway shut. She let go of Od's wrist and Od flung herself away. She almost fell, but didn't somehow, then she shut the suitcase and held it shut as she ran and stumbled for the door. She could hear Mrs. Scrobe coming for her. Her feet thundering into the ground as she made it to a full stand, her screaming getting louder at Od's back. Od grabbed the door and threw it open. She could feel something between her shoulder blades. Then she was through the door and a horrible crash came from behind. But Od didn't look. She *ran.*

She ran down the twisted hallway, too slowly because of the

suitcase, sure that one of the doors would open and the Scrobe boys would drag her back, or maybe they'd be hiding behind one of the turns and she would crash into them and it would be all over. She went through the dark living room with the static too loud on the TV and opened the door. She was sure that Gatch would be standing in the doorway, or Corlan, or Thad, or Bray, or even their dad that she had never seen nor heard much of—one of them would have been summoned to catch her. But in reality, no one was there. She ran down the driveway and the creepiness of Wisner, through Bob's property and to her house. The entire time she was sure somebody would get her. Her heart was punching the inside of her chest and in her head. Hard. Fast. And then she found herself inside, in her own kitchen on her knees over the suitcase. Her hair was stuck to her face. Her lungs burned. Her arms and legs throbbed and wobbled. What had she done?

When she could finally pull herself off the floor, Od found that N was empty. No Bernie. No Loney. No Ed's Body. No Emily Cline.

28

LITTLE BOXES

OD DRANK TWO GLASSES of water before she searched N and found it empty. Then she gathered up the suitcase and her backpack and climbed aboard the Grand National. She drove slow through the mountain roads, scanning the hills and trees, dark driveways and abandoned front porches, as she drove towards the graveyard.

Why had Loney left? Had his brothers taken him back to his house? She hoped he was all right. And hopefully those pills knocked Mrs. Scrobe out…although once the brothers found their mom lying on the floor of her bedroom, they might just come for Od anyway.

And where had Bernie gone? Did he just bail or did he follow Ed's Body and Emily Cline somewhere? Just as she had the thought Od saw the pair outside Katie Cooper's house, down and across the street from the cemetery. Od pulled the Grand National past them and then ran back to Katie's. The Coopers had a picket fence, a white one, just like the movies, and Bernie, Ed's Body, and Emily Cline were sitting with their backs against it. None of them got up when she got there either. Bernie just looked up and said, "Hi."

"What the hell?" Od said throwing her hands in the air.

"So," Bernie said, "Ed's Body and Emily had had enough of the house and just left, pretty much right after you did. I tried to grab her hand and pull them back, but they were both resisting, like supernatural-strength resisting. They pulled free and walked out the door. So I ran after them and grabbed Emily's hand and pulled them back as hard as I could. And, well..." Bernie reached into his jeans pocket and pulled out a finger. "Emily's finger came off."

Od gaped at the finger. *He kept that in his pocket.*

"So then I just kind of followed them...until I got the idea to grab them and tie them to this fence." Bernie smiled.

They *were* tied to the fence—or Emily was, rather. With the string from Bernie's hoodie, it looked like.

"What's up with you?" Bernie asked. He stuffed the finger back into his front jeans pocket.

"Nothing, just drugged Loney's mom. I also stole a box of souls, a pair of ghost goggles, and some metal gloves."

"Cool."

"Where's Loney?"

"I don't know. He never came back from talking with his brothers."

"How are we going to get these two back to the house?"

"I don't know. Maybe we could tie them up and throw them in the car."

"I doubt it. Ed's Body doesn't like to be grabbed. Have you tried it?"

"No, for this I just kind of ran around the corner and right as Emily was next to the fence I wrapped my hoodie string around her arm and then around the fence real quick. I thought for a second that she might just pull off her arm and keep going, but she stopped and so did Ed's Body when it felt her stop, you know, 'cause they were still holding hands. Then they kind of stood here for a while until I sat down and then they sat down a little while ago."

"They're probably heading back to the graveyard."

Bernie looked down the street toward the graveyard. "Yeah, that's why I tied them. Thought they might go back into the Mausoleum of the Living Dead." Bernie used a spooky voice and did his creepy finger thing.

"So you tied them up in Katie's front yard."

"Katie Cooper?"

Oh god. "Yeah."

"This is Katie Cooper's house?"

"Yes."

Bernie looked up at the house in awe. *Awe.* As if a cheerleader's house was more amazing than what he had witnessed tonight. More amazing than a room of half-rotted corpses coming to life. "Which room is hers?" He was practically grinning.

"Bernie, that isn't the point."

But he wasn't listening. "Is it the one in the front at the top? I bet it is."

"Bernie."

"What?"

"There are more important things…and they're tied to the fence."

"I love her, Od."

Oh god. "I'm sure you do, but we have to figure some other things out."

"She's right *there.*"

"Where?" Od spun around expecting to see her friend.

"Right in that house. She's right in there. Probably in there dreaming of undead unicorns and dragon skeletons come to life."

Od sighed. "Bernie..." She bit the inside of her cheek and tugged at the waist of her jeans. "What would a hero do?"

"He would go get her."

"No, a hero would put his personal stuff aside to save the

masses from the risen corpses and restore his cousin's soul to his body."

Bernie looked at that front right window at the top of the Cooper's house and sighed. "So, now what? What now? How?"

"I don't know, Hero. Figure it out."

He sat down next to Ed's Body and Emily Cline and came up with nothing.

After a while Loney stumbled up with dirt on his face and a leaf stuck in his hair. The front of his shirt soaked through with blood.

"Oh my God! Loney!"

"I'm, uh, OK now."

"What did they do?"

Loney lifted his hand and pulled the neck of his shirt down to show her the thick metal shaft sticking out about an inch above his clavicle, and about an inch out of his skin. It was not unlike the one Od still had stuck in her. Although it protruded more. "My soul won't leave my body now when I go into the graveyard." Loney touched the metal rod where it met his skin and squinted. "It's an anchor."

"That's gnarly, dude," Bernie said, sniffing and rubbing his nose with the sleeve of his hoodie.

"That's what they wanted?"

"Yup." Loney looked over at Ed's Body. "Guess they were trying to help."

"Help?" Bernie laughed.

"What about you? How'd it go with my mom?"

"Well, I got a pair of gloves and goggles that interact with souls or ghosts or whatever. And…a… uh…a soul box."

Loney raised an eyebrow. "She let you take that stuff?"

"No. Some of it she was going to let me take though."

"How'd you get it?"

"I...well, first let me say that we should all be on the lookout for your brothers. 'Cause I'm not sure how long the pills really last." Loney just stared at her. Blank. "I shoved a bunch of those sleeping pills into her mouth and made her eat them. Then I grabbed all the stuff and ran."

"What?! Why?" Loney followed her as she went back to the Grand National.

"No way was she going to let me have the souls. I tried to get more, but the bed collapsed. They're trapped in those little boxes. There were tons of them under her bed. It wasn't just the one she used with me. We need to free them." Od pulled the suitcase from the back of the car and threw it onto the back of the car.

"Od, how are you going to do that? Don't you think that she would have let them go if she could?" Loney was watching everything she was doing.

"No. I think she uses them for stuff. Like making other souls. And prolly worse stuff." Od unzipped the suitcase and flipped open the top. She found the goggles and pulled them over her head. She adjusted the strap so that it fit snugly and then set them just above her hairline.

"How are you going to release them?"

Od grabbed the gauntlets. They felt heavier. "I was planning on just smashing the box."

"What? What if that kills them all?"

"...I don't think it will."

"But what if it does?"

"It's better than being trapped. I mean, what if they are like fusing together and losing their identities, or just slowly breaking down? Souls are what are left when we die, right? So smashing something physical like the box shouldn't kill them. It will just break the prison."

"Then what? They have to go somewhere."

"Yeah, they'll go to the afterlife or haunt some place. I mean, what happens when you die outside? You don't need somebody to put your soul in a box or something."

"Why do I feel like I'm Peter Venkman telling you not to shut the protection grid down?"

"I can't let them be trapped forever."

"What about Ed?"

"He'd do the same. We can put him back too."

"This is all a bad idea."

Od finished putting the gauntlets on. She buckled them to fit her hands and snapped the back covers in place. Then she put the soul box in the center of the street and got the Grand National. She took a deep breath, put the car in gear and leaned on the gas. The front driver's side tire hit the box square and crushed it. She braked, rolled back over the box for good measure, and turned off the engine, then she slid the goggles over her eyes. A hundred little Ms. Pac-Man ghosts swam into the night. Up and out. Through the trees. They were a great array of faded colors. She reached out and grabbed a pink one with the gauntlets. It squirmed in her grip, twisted and pulled away into the night.

"Here." Od handed the goggles to Loney.

Loney looked. "Jeez, if Pac-Man had nightmares..."

"Lemme see."

Loney handed the goggles to Bernie.

"See," Od said to Loney.

"Still doesn't get us any closer to getting Ed back in his proper body."

"But now I know the goggles and gauntlets work and this took, what, two minutes?"

"Uh-oh." Bernie stared into the dark with the goggles still strapped to his head.

Od and Loney turned.

"What?"

"They're dying," Bernie said. "They're just…dying."

Od grabbed the goggles away from him and put them to her face. The ghosts were falling through the trees to the ground. Some still skipped across the sky, but more and more fell. Dying, just like Bernie had said. *What was wrong with them? What have I done...?* And then she saw. They weren't dying. They weren't falling. They were diving. Into the cemetery. "Oh shit." She tore the goggles from her eyes. *What have I done?*

"OK, I'm open to suggestions."

Od looked from Loney to Bernie. She felt helpless.

"What's going on?"

"I may have royally fucked up." She tried a smile on, but the expression didn't feel like it fit. "Apparently… the souls are going into the graves." She said it rationally but only gained blank stares from Loney and Bernie. So she spelled it out. "You know...for the bodies."

"Oh shit," the two boys said in unison.

"Yeah, so we have however long it takes for somebody to dig their way out of a grave before we are dealing with a massive undead horde."

They all stood there for a good thirty seconds waiting for their minds to completely wrap around the situation they had been thrown into.

"What about the scarebox?"

"It won't work," said Loney.

"Why not? It has already, a few times."

"It didn't work on Od," said Bernie.

"I don't think pushing souls out of bodies is what a scarebox is meant for. The scarebox pushed my soul out because it's loose. I know that because my soul had already come out on its own when I was in Devotion with Ed's Body earlier," said Loney. "I think it pushed Ed's out because his was loose too, because he was calming N down. Scareboxes are very powerful, but the most it can scare at once can't be more than four or five souls, and that's probably stretching it. And they have to be close to the box for it to work on them."

"But these souls probably *are* loose in those dead people."

"Od!" That was Ed's voice.

Od swung around.

It was Ed in Ed's own body...being Ed. He turned one of the corners of his mouth up in that smile only he could make. She ran at him and threw her arms around him. He was back somehow. In his own body. She was laughing and crying with her face buried in his shoulder, then she was gagging on the stench of death that stuck to him and she pulled away.

"What? How?" Od said.

"Holy crap are those long answers," said Ed. "I saw souls. The gray ones, a hundred I think, maybe more. I don't know. But I felt them from the church so came out here through the tunnels. FYI, as a ghost—for me anyway—going outside is like going into a blizzard. A ripping, thrashing, fuck-storm of energy with shit flying from everywhere. I barely got here—barely and blindly. I had to follow the pull which led me to my body." He stopped and looked down. "It wanted me inside it. It has been pulling all night. I didn't know that was what it was, and I was resisting it. I'm so stupid."

"I don't know what the fuck you just said," replied Bernie. "But the dead are about to rise from their graves. So glad to have you back, but we've got problems—"

"The dead?" said Ed.

"Yeah, all those souls you saw went into the graves, into the bodies in the graves, so we'll be dealing with them. Fairly shortly," added Od.

"Sounds like you have some long answers too," said Ed.

"I have an idea," said Loney.

"Loony?" said Ed. They looked at each other. Ed wasn't even trying to hide his disdain for the other boy.

"You wouldn't be here in your own body if it wasn't for him," said Od.

"That's true," Bernie said. "He's better than people think."

Ed and Loney exchanged looks. Then Ed looked back at Od. "Where did all the souls come from?"

"A soul box…it's a long story too, so we can tell stories later."

Loney turned to Od. "Let's break it."

"What?"

"The scarebox. Let's break it."

"What? Why?"

"Cross the streams," Bernie said to himself.

"The scarebox has an enormous amount of power—or harnesses it, anyway. It only focuses a small part of it through the opening when you press the button. If we were to smash it in the center of the graveyard, I think there is a good chance that it will release all of the energy in all directions. Like a bomb. It should be enough to push the souls back out of their bodies. Since Ed is back, we don't need it to try and get back into his body. I won't leave my body 'cause I have the anchors. And you and Bernie probably won't be affected since your souls aren't loose."

"*Probably*?" said Bernie.

"Yeah, but when we do that where will they go? Can't they just go back into the dead?" Od asked.

"Or into *us*. Remember that possibility?" Bernie interjected.

"So we need a place to put them," said Loney.

Od knew exactly where to put them. "Put them in me," she said.

"What the fuck?!" said Ed.

"No way," said Loney.

"Where else can we put them?" Really, if they had another idea she would love to hear it.

"I vote we leave them in the dead people and let the town deal with it," said Bernie.

"I agree with Bernie," said Ed. He smiled. Od thought that he really would like to see how that played out. She may have secretly liked to see that as well…but the consequences wouldn't be worth it, and responsibility weighed upon her.

"I did this. I *have* to make it right. I can't leave them like this," she said.

"What harm would it do?" said Loney.

"Uh, they could kill people, make people go crazy, or who knows. It would obviously be bad," said Od. "You've seen movies before, haven't you?"

"Maybe people should know this. Isn't covering it up, or 'fixing it'… almost like lying?"

"No. It's fixing something I did wrong that could hurt somebody. Even if it just hurt one person…killed one person..."

"We couldn't even get them into you," said Loney.

"I have a spout. Your mom put it in me. It can funnel them into me." She pulled the neck her shirt aside to show the fat needle in her lower neck. "Twinsies," she said to Loney.

"Yeah, but then what? Would you just have hundreds of different half-souls fighting to take control of you from the inside?"

"I had nine of them go through me before and didn't feel a thing. How I understand it is that it's not really *in* me anyway— they're attached to me, like they're haunting me. They can't control my body. I didn't even know they were there before." Some of that might have been contrary to what Mrs. Scrobe said, but that didn't matter right now; they could deal with what-ifs later.

"There have to be some kind of repercussions," said Loney.

"This is a bad idea," said Bernie.

"I'll deal with the side effects."

"How do we get them to the funnel though?" Ed said.

"We need a beacon," said Od.

"A what?" said Bernie.

"A *beacon*. You know, something to lure them into the funnel. Like a lighthouse for the undead. Something shiny to attract them and lure them in."

"Can we use the gloves and goggles? You know, grab them and push them in?" Bernie said. They were coming around to her idea now. She was hoping one of them could talk her out of it.

"Maybe… but there's probably too many. A hundred of them or so. Going in every direction."

Ed's eyes lit up, then darkened. "I have something... but I have to go get it," said Ed. "I have to be out of my body though." Ed looked at his sister. There was a sadness, *and* a proudness there. "I don't know what is going on, but I trust Od. If she thinks this is the best way…" Ed looked into her eyes and she looked back into his.

They all stood there in silence.

Od sighed. And finally nodded.

"There's a light. A bright stone…probably not a real stone, since it isn't physical. It looks like The Light...you know, the one you're supposed to see when you die. It'll attract them, I think. It pulls souls to it. I felt it."

Od looked at her brother. "Don't get lost this time. Come right back to your body."

"I will."

29

DEAD END

ED CLOSED HIS EYES and tried to click into the graveyard like he had done with N so many times before. It was different. Sour. Kind of sweet too, but not a good sweet. Apparently, this would loosen his soul so that it could be pushed out like at their house. He could see Od opening the box, and then the rage of the scarebox threw his soul backwards and into another rage: the outside world. It was a never-ending blizzard against his naked soul.

Below him he could see the half-souls, as Od had called them, pushing up towards him, glowing gray smudges trying to find life. Her trudged through the graveyard to the church next door. The outside torrent quit as he burled through the carved front doors of the church. Inside was the ghost cult, clumped together and chanting. He moved through the pews and up to the dais where the shimmering cross rose above everything save the dark-stained windows. The light-stone was there, under a pale blanket, at the base of the cross where it had fallen, marking the life and soul he had obliterated. He still felt as if he should have paid for doing that, some sort of penance or punishment, but there was nothing that he could think of that would cover it. He grabbed it and the church ghosts stopped chanting and turned their dull glowing eyes on him. Ed stopped.

"It is not yours." The Are said.

"It is more mine than yours," said Ed.

"It is not the Are. It is for the cross. For the others. It is what is done."

"It's mine." Ed moved toward the doors.

The Are came apart and went for him. They were faster than he thought and they surrounded him. He held the stone close, tucked into his chest, as they fell on him. Their limbs didn't have any digits; they just soaked him up. He could feel himself in many of them at once, a cold foreign feeling, and a sense of their vague individuality at each point they touched him. He got lost in each of those feelings, tasting each in turn and then all at once. It was like a complex meal created by a chef. There was salt, and pepper, and spice, and meat, and blood… as they strapped him to the cross once more. The clear straps bound him tighter than before. Crueler.

It was harder to see the mirrors and ponds that reflected off the other souls this time. Was it because of the harsh bindings? He wasn't sure he could find the tunnels; things didn't seem to line up like last time. The Are were still binding him tighter and the tunnels were slipping away. He had the stone still clutched to his chest. They would take it when they finished binding him, but he still had it now. It was a chance…a reflection caught him…and through the cluster of ghosts that were fixed around him he saw a single tunnel through himself.

OD PUT THE SCAREBOX where she thought the center of the graveyard must be. It was at the intersection of the two tiny roads. Ed's Body sat shotgun with Emily Cline. It was like it was before Ed came back, thank god—none of them had been entirely sure that the body wouldn't just keel over and die this time. In fact, it didn't even cross her mind before she had opened the scarebox again.

She had put the box about fifteen feet from front driver's side tire, so she could see it over the dash, and get up enough speed to break it. The black-mirror goggles were strapped to her head and pulled over her eyes, so that she could see when Ed's ghost came back. That is when she would crush it. If she did so before he got there, the souls might get too far away and they might never get them back. Or they might re-infest the dead again, and they'd never be able to get them out. After the box was destroyed she would get out of the car and stand in the headlights and wait for Ed to lure all of the souls into her. Then he would jump back into his body. Then they would go home. And she would keep the goggles and gauntlets on until this whole thing was done. That way she could see Ed stand next to the box and make sure every soul was caught.

Beneath her she could see fuzzy images of the Pac-Man ghosts moving, this time slowly upwards. It was strange that she could see them even though they were inside bodies now. When she pointed the goggles at Loney and Bernie she didn't see anything. Hopefully Ed returned before they broke ground. He had said that time moved differently in the "Pale." Weird—that was the word she called it in her head too, when she visited through her dream.

Bernie and Loney were across the street at Lane Market, just as a precaution. Sure, Loney apparently had an "anchor" that made his soul stay put, but who knew how well that thing worked, and Bernie had never been exposed to the scarebox at a close distance. Od was certain her own soul would stay put, though—it had so far. *Here's spittin' in the Devil's eye.*

There was a flash of bright from behind. Like a camera flash or lighting, only lasting a tad longer and closer to the ground. Od looked up into the rearview, then back through the rear windshield.

As she turned, the light returned. It was a car. Od kept an eye on it, waiting for it to pass the graveyard. Probably somebody going to work at this ungodly hour. But it didn't pass. It was slowing down. It was turning into the graveyard. She didn't have the motor on, or the headlights, but it looked as if the car was heading right toward her.

"OD!" It was Loney.

Shit. Should she run the box over? Or get out and see what he was screaming about? He wouldn't just yell like that for nothing.

"WHAT THE FUCK??" That was Bernie.

The car had stopped just inside the graveyard. Ed's ghost was nowhere to be seen.

Fuck. She turned the key in the ignition and threw the Grand National into reverse, cranked the wheel to get out of the path of the box, and drove around it. Once clear of the scarebox, she gunned it, driving up on the grass and nearly clipping a headstone. Wind whipped in through her open window as she accelerated towards the new car. Ed's Body was just looking out the window, uninterested in what was going on. It seemed to be enjoying the speed. It even looked over at her…*with a smile? Was that a smile?* She was on a different road than the new car, she realized, and she was heading out to the main street. Good, she could come up behind it. She looked around. *Where was Loney?* She got out onto Crest, slammed the car into park and jumped out, searching for Loney or Bernie or maybe for whoever had driven the--

--a bright light exploded from nowhere and was gone as soon as it appeared…silver flecks flicked across the night...

--there were trees. Graves. The night sky. The road. What was going on? *Did I get out of the car...?*

--somebody was yelling somewhere. The headlights of the Grand National were throwing huge shadows behind such tiny rocks on the road...*Am I on the ground...?* She must have been hit by something—by someone she hadn't seen…

--There were two red eyes staring from the dark—glowing eyes floating beyond the dirt that had been kicked up into dust. No. Not eyes. Taillights from the car. The *other* car…

--Od could see people, and she could see what they were doing, but she couldn't form a connection from them or their actions to anything in her mind. She looked on, untethered.

Loney was there in the dust, grappling with somebody in the harsh headlights of the Grand National. Legs went back and forth before her, but she couldn't focus on them. Bernie swam out of the dark and then fell a foot from her. It seemed to happen both near and far away. Blood splashed out of his mouth. Loud red blood with thick black shadows behind it. He was groaning. Od was finding her feet. Standing on them. *That's what you did with them.* Her head thumped with each heartbeat. Hard. Painful. The world was moving in strange ways. Blurring, kind of. No, blurring was the wrong word. It was just a lack of focus.

Loney hit somebody, but then another person grabbed him from behind. Od started for him, but something grabbed *her* from behind. Then she saw, and felt stupid that she didn't know that it was the Scrobe brothers all along. Of course it was them. It was weird that there was enough time for her to feel stupid. Everything was happening all at once now. There was something going into her mouth. Something dirty. Movies told her it was a gag, and it was being tied way too tight by movie standards. It stretched and split her lips. She saw Loney had one too. Blood was running down his face. Corlan and Bray had Loney. Thad had her. And it looked like Bernie had taken out Gatch.

The Scrobe boys were all shoving them towards their car. A Plymouth or Pontiac. Gold and black. Similar to her parent's car. Loney was being dragged, mostly. Od thought she was fighting back hard, but her head hurt and her arms felt like they were full of rocks. She was drooling around the gag and her lips were bleeding. Ed's Body stared at them from the dark front passenger seat of the Grand National; it was with the dead girl. She couldn't come up with her name. Od screamed "help" at them, but the scream had no volume and hurt her throat. The gag caught all the letters she was trying to make.

They got Loney to the car first, but he was fighting. He had his feet up on the side of the car and was pushing with his legs and twisting his body. He broke free. He was flailing at his brothers, as bits of his adrenaline poked through. His movements were crazed and exhausted. Od tried to get away too, but for some reason she couldn't think straight enough to figure it out. Loney hit both of the brothers that had been holding him and knocked one of them to the ground. He ran towards her, stumbling from the speed, and then crashed to the ground. He got up again but—

Gatch tripped him and he hit the ground face first. His hands must have been tied behind his back. He lifted his head and Od saw the new gashes the ground made, blood running like tears. He started to say something, but Gatch was behind him with a big chunk of cement. He brought it down hard on top of Loney's head. The first hit took all the tension out of his neck, all of the resistance out of his body. His limbs stopped working and he fell, but Gatch kept hitting, making a series of dull, wet *thunks* with the cement. Od was screaming through the gag, a muffled sound that made an unharmonious marriage with the noise Gatch was creating from his brother's skull.

Bray and Corlan pulled Gatch away, flecks of blood dotting his face and painting his hands which still held the dripping chunk of cinder. It had been for just a second, but right before his brothers dropped him into their trunk and shut the lid, Od saw Gatch close his eyes, inhale deep, and smile. Loney was still. His face was glued to the ground in a collection of his own blood. Od wasn't sure if it was her vision failing her, or if it was actually happening, but it looked like Loney's arm was moving spastically. It felt as if sanity was escaping from her. Tears smeared her vision. She couldn't figure out how to work her body. She was screaming. Screaming for her lack of control. Screaming into the dirty rag that ate up the sound. That is when the undead came.

AT FIRST OD THOUGHT the commotion had caused everybody in the neighborhood to come outside, even though they were pretty far from the houses. There were dark shapes, man shapes, behind the car, and coming silently...but that wasn't right. If it was people, they would be talking or yelling or running, and they should be coming from the street, not the cemetery. No, these weren't people. They were the half-souled undead. A few at first, but then there were more…and more. The Scrobes didn't see them, initially. They were all talking in scrambled *wah-wah-wahs*. They should have been calling 9-1-1, or driving Loney to a hospital for an IV or surgery or something, but they weren't doing that. It looked as if they were arguing without actually talking to each other.

They didn't see the walking corpses until they broke into the light. And when they did see them, they just stood unmoving and confused…frowning at them until the few turned to a dozen. Until the dozen doubled. Now the things were reaching for the Scrobe boys, and the way that they clawed at them looked as if they were trying to get inside them—as if they weren't used to having their new bodies and were still trying to find a home. Once they realized what was happening it didn't take long for the Scrobe brothers to scratch their way through the undead and get into their car. Too bad it hadn't taken them another few minutes, because at that point the undead had doubled again and Od didn't think that they could have escaped that many. But the Scrobe boys did escape, and they drove away as fast as they could.

Od was on the ground again, only she didn't remember falling. Her shoulder hurt now. She tried to move her arms and realized that her wrists had been tied behind her. She pulled and the rope loosened. She pulled harder, feeling the blood bulge in the skin of her hands, and then the hasty knot gave and came away. She got up and wobbled toward where she thought Loney was, but there were so many walking corpses that she couldn't tell where that was anymore. As she edged forward the things turned towards her, so she backpedaled and stumbled back to the Grand National.

She climbed in through the driver's door and fired up the engine. It made a terrible noise—it must have been already on, she was just grinding the gears. She squeezed her eyes shut and opened them again, shaking her head, trying to get back to normal. Then she put the car in reverse and flipped it around to go back up the tiny road she had come down on. *If Loney was alive*...she was heading for the scarebox...*Please let Ed's ghost be there*. She had lost the goggles somewhere so she wouldn't be able to see if he was there before she crushed it. Ed's Body stuck its head out the window as they drove, like a happy dog. Emily Cline sat next to it, staring at nothing. Dead people were everywhere and she was hitting them right and left. Limbs caught on her side-views. Faces smashed against the windshield. They jerked the steering wheel and pulled the car each time she hit one, threatening to make her crash. The movies didn't tell her that would happen.

Something was blocking the headlights now, but whatever it was came away just in time for Od to see the scarebox and turn the wheel, crushing it beneath the front driver's side tire. A deep boom ran through the car, loud and sudden. She felt it whip through the car. Through her innards. Bodies dropped all around her, falling right where they stood.

She slammed the brakes, got out of the car and knelt at the door, searching for the goggles on the floorboards. They weren't there. She climbed back behind the wheel and hung her head upside down to look underneath the seat. Something fell over her face and caught on her ears. The goggles. They must have been hanging around her neck. She pulled them up to her eyes and looked around.

Little Ms. Pac-Man ghosts were flying up and away, scattering like campfire embers. One of them came towards her. It had something like a star at the center of it...*that must be the Light thing*. And this must be Ed. She saw him come closer to her and then so close that he was just an unfocused jumble of color. That star, though…that soul-light stayed true and came so close to her that it almost blinded her, and then suddenly she couldn't see it anymore. All of the souls came to her then. They floated in from everywhere and when they got so close that they became a pixelated mess, they disappeared from her sight. She swung around to see if they had been merely going through her, but none were leaving—they only came. They must be attaching to her. She stepped backward as they came and they followed her, she moved to the side and they moved with her. So she ran, knowing they would follow.

She ran as fast as she could, dodging gravestones and family mausoleums, hurdling dead bodies, skeletal remains, and mounds of dirt as best she could. It all melted into the darkness and fell behind her. Trees and roads weren't there. Only Loney, who was lying in the road very close to the graves. It took a little bit of searching before she found him. He was at the center of a bunch of bodies, half buried beneath them, but she found him. And when she pulled the other dead bodies off of him, it was obvious that he was dead. Blood had pooled around him. His skin was torn and parts of his clothes were shredded. The back of his head was ruined. She flipped him over, hoping that his face would contradict what she already knew, but it only solidified it. With his eyes. They were staring eyes. Broken doll eyes. She was staring too, with what felt like broken eyes, because how could somebody see such a thing. One of his eyes was slightly crooked and they both didn't blink. She would remember them forever. His staring—unstaring—eyes.

She put the goggles back on, which had fallen back around her neck as she ran. She saw the souls continue to pour into her. There weren't many of them left; these were the slow ones, the stragglers. She watched them peripherally, unable to focus her eyes on anything. Dull colors swimming through the trees, growing as they came towards her and then winking out when they got too close. Colors in the night. Her mind wouldn't focus either. She just stared at nothing until the last of the colors melted into her. She didn't know how long she had been standing there when she blinked and saw Ed's Body standing next to her. It had followed her there. It must have. It went over and sat next to Loney's body. She pulled the goggles off.

"Holy shit!" That was Bernie. "Did we win?" She had forgotten about her cousin in the chaos. Shame swam into the emptiness inside her, playing emotional tricks that she had never felt before.

Od just stared. It was like floating on the ocean. She had stayed up all night with Katie once—it was like that. Like the next night when she was still up. Everything was there, but not. Things were different, but not at all. Weird, but the same. She didn't have much left in her.

Bernie found Loney and said something. Maybe he cried. Maybe not. She doubted it. Ed's Body sat there. They all sat there for a long time—minutes, hours, surely not that long—but time didn't really exist anymore. Then Ed was back.

"Aghhh... my head," said Ed.

Od grabbed him and hugged his nasty dead-smelling body,

trembling. He hugged her back.

She did what she set out to do. But…she lost.

"Ed," was all she could say.

"We have to get the Grand National back before Bob notices. And we have to get out of here." Ed was right.

"We have to get Loney's body back to the Scrobes."

"No."

"Ed, we have to…"

"He wouldn't want that."

"How would you know?"

There was a long silence until 'Ed' broke it. "'Cause I'm him."

She looked at her brother. "What?"

"I'm Loney."

"I—what?"

"I was trapped. The anchor kept me in my body even as those things were tearing me open, trying to get in me. I could feel it, but I was dead. I couldn't move any bit of my body, but I couldn't leave either. I could feel it all…Ed saw me and pulled me out. He put me in his body. Said that I needed to look after you." He looked into her eyes. His were so wet, helpless, and sad. "He said that his body was rejecting him, that he couldn't get back into it. But I'm…" Loney-Ed trailed off, abandoning that last thought to his own mind.

"…what?"

"He said that he was going to attach to you. Actually, it was like he told me without talking—sorry, not that that matters. He wants to keep the half-souls from trying to take you over… He's…haunting you, in a good way. Kinda being part of you, to keep you safe."

Od didn't say anything. She didn't know how to feel. She didn't know what she felt. Sadness, definitely…Anger, for sure…But for some reason, relief…? Shame…There were other emotions there as well…She couldn't fit her mind around it. She needed Ed. Her twin.

"Maybe he'll visit your dreams," said Bernie.

It was possible. She knew it was possible. But without Mrs. Scrobe it would be more difficult. *Jeez…What about the Scrobes? What was Mrs. Scrobe going to do?*

Dawn was breaking.

She hugged Loney-Ed.

Then she hugged Bernie. Tight. He seemed embarrassed by it.

"Ed," Od said, feeling small. There was so much to say…but there wasn't anything she could say then. She wanted to hug *him*. Then she felt for the Spout at the bottom of her neck and twisted it like Mrs. Scrobe said to do after you attached the souls to keep them in place.

And they all sat down there between the road and the cemetery.

"Man, look at that," Bernie said staring out over the dimly lit sea of dead bodies. A faint light was rising in the sky, revealing the holes scattered across the graveyard. "Kind of wish I had my camera."

THEY ALL LOOKED out over the graves and bodies and trees.

"OD," said Bernie. Then he handed her something soft...a pair of striped underwear? It didn't make any sense, but it tugged at something in her memory. *Damn,* she thought. *Mom and Dad are going to be home in a few hours and I still need to clean my room.*

Od
AND
Ed

ACKNOWLEDGMENTS

I have a lot of people to thank. Frist, a big special thanks to William F. Reed IV. Without that fool this book might not be in your hands right now. I like that guy. Big thanks to Ben Schyan, his generosity is king and he is a good friend. Special Thanks to Shastina Leonard, Cristian Bruce, Berrenda Fox, Brenda Sue Sponsler, Brenda Leonard, Dr. William S. Leonard, Jennifer Buffo, "Brasso", Kimra Bennett, Nissa Spurlin, Nikki Leere, Frank "MVP" McLaughlin, Tom Provost, Joshua Davis, Samantha McDougal, Chad "Wesley Cash" Matthews. A giant thank you to the whole Miskovsky clan: Jason, Amy, Lauren, and especially Kate, who was the first to give Od a real voice. Special Thanks to Amanda Goodrich, Anderson "Friendo" William, Carina Chadwick, Diego "Budso" Garcia, Rachel Ramirez, Kathy Pritchett, Jennifer Giandalone, Alexx Wells, Rebecca Trotter, Gabrielle Yates, Kelly Monser, Sean Fetters, Jeffrey Sherman, Cara B. Buckley, Marissa Kilgore, Heidi Von Muldorfer, Jacob Adams, Rory Christiansen, Jessica Lamb, Charity Whyte, Matthew "Mratt" Pritchett, Sari Karplus, Jennifer Juvenelle, Evan Michael Hart, Megan Sherman, Nicole Klemens, Michael Lombardo, Brian Sylva, Rudeboy Pictures, and Duck Industries. Y'all rock. And a big ol' thank you to Stephanie Cohen whose insightfulness was invaluable.

ABOUT THE AUTHOR

Shanti grew up in a tiny town in the mountains of Northern California, riding bikes and sleds, and playing in the forest surrounding his house.

Many people who live in his hometown claim some sort of experience with the supernatural. He remains skeptical... with many unexplained experiences of his own.

Od and Ed's story does not end here.